PATRICIA POWELL was born in Jamaica in 1966, and lived there until 1982, when she emigrated to the United States. She received her B.A. in English Literature from Wellesley College, Massachusetts in 1988, and at the same time received Departmental Honours for the completion of *Me Dying Trial*, published by Heinemann in 1993. Excerpts from the novel appeared in *The Boston Phoenix Literary Supplement* (December 1987), and in *The Caribbean Writer* (Spring 1990). In 1991 Powell received her M.F.A. in Creative Writing, Fiction, from Brown University in Rhode Island. While at Brown University she completed this, her second novel, *A Small Gathering of Bones*. An excerpt from this novel appeared in *Art and Understanding: The International Magazine of Literature and Arts about AIDS* (Summer 1992). She is currently Assistant Professor of Creative Writing at the University of Massachusetts, Boston.

PATRICIA POWELL

A SMALL GATHERING
OF BONES

Heinemann

Heinemann Educational Publishers
A Division of Heinemann Publishers (Oxford) Ltd
Halley Court, Jordan Hill, Oxford OX2 8EJ

Heinemann: A Division of Reed Publishing (USA) Inc.
361 Hanover Street, Portsmouth, NH 03801–3912, USA

Heinemann Educational Books (Nigeria) Ltd
PMB 5205, Ibadan
Heinemann Educational Boleswa
PO Box 10103, Village Post Office, Gaborone, Botswana

FLORENCE   PRAGUE   PARIS   MADRID
ATHENS   MELBOURNE   JOHANNESBURG
AUCKLAND   SINGAPORE   TOKYO
CHICAGO   SAO PAULO

First published by Heinemann Educational Publishers in 1994

Series Editor: Adewale Maja-Pearce

British Library Cataloguing in Publication Data
A catalogue record for this book is available from the British Library.

ISBN 0435 989 367

Cover design by Touchpaper
Cover illustration by Jane Human
Author photograph by Ananda Lowe

Phototypeset by CentraCet Limited, Cambridge
Printed and bound in Great Britain
by Cox & Wyman Ltd, Reading, Berkshire

94   95   96   97   10   9   8   7   6   5   4   3   2   1

In Memory of I. Facey
(1963–1989)

A Million Thanks to
Graduate Fellows in my Fiction Classes at Brown University (1989–1991);
Professors Meredith Steinbach, Michael Ondaatje, Ed White;
And as always, Teresa Langle de Paz

February 1978

When Ian Kaysen first come down with the offensive dry cough, Dale did have to finally tell him one Saturday morning, as him watch Ian stumble into the kitchen rubbing his chest, back hunched over: 'Ian Kaysen, I don't mean to interfere in your personal prerogatives, but that rattle in that back of your throat not any little play-play cold. You going to have to do something about that coughing. Maybe your resistance is low. Eat more fruit and vegetables. Quit the blasted cigarette smoking!' Dale cry out, voice a little bit on edge, as him raise off the couch where him spend the night, and follow the long slender fellow into the kitchen. 'Sleep in your own bed when night come down! Stop hackle-hackle your body!'

For what frighten Dale the most, as him watch Ian seated near the window, two fluffy pillows prop-up behind him, was that it wasn't just any ordinary coughing that start off with a tickling at the back of the throat and finish off a little later with a few ke-hem, ke-hem, a harsh nose-blow and a sound wipe. It wasn't the kind either that would retreat after a tall glass of water, two aspirins or even a mug full of busy tea steamed for several hours. It was like the devil from hell inside him want to come out, but the walls of his throat it seems, just too narrow.

'My little cousins used to come down with all kinds of ailments,' Dale give out, as him half-full a glass tumbler from out the cabinet with castor oil; 'whooping cough, gingivitis, colic, dengue. But I never see anything like this.' Him shake his head slow from side to side, speckles of the day's growth of hair already shadowing his mahogany face, the round scar in the middle of his forehead that

1

resemble the hardened back of a seven-day-old land crab pulsing vigorously.

'My mother used to make us drink this thing. Maybe it will help.' Him reach into the fridge for two of the limes, for Nevin like his lemonade make from scratch, and after rolling them few times on the floor, under his stout, heavy foot, to soften them, him rinse them under the hot water and squeeze them into the tumbler. 'The castor oil,' Dale continue on, slightly out of breath, as him stir the heavy liquid with a tall thin spoon, 'will coat the walls of your throat. With all that coughing, them bound to sore up. And the lime juice will kill the germs.'

But as Dale turn around to hand Ian the tumbler, him notice the fellow curved over, head resting on chest fast asleep, thin arms stretch out by his side. The racket in his chest did stop and his breathing seem calm and easy. The light morning breeze blowing in through the half-open windows was tugging at the yellow curtains Dale put up only last week and teasing the tiny curls on Ian's head.

Dale sigh long and deep before resting the tumbler softly on the counter. Him couldn't decide whether to wake Ian. Him was so innocent-looking lying there with thick, bushy eyebrows that meet in the middle and long lashes that don't curve. Half Indian, him say when Dale ask what him mix with. And not Indian from India either, him endeavour to clarify, but Arawak Indian. The real thing. Dale did smile. That was when Ian's charcoal eyes used to tremble like jewels and there was a bounce in each of his footsteps. When his father was still alive, and him and the mother used to talk. Now it seems as if him losing weight, the way his wrist look smaller and more limp and the way his fingers seem longer and bonier. The gold band on the thumb of his left hand didn't seem loose atall, though; or his clothes for that matter.

And that Saturday morning, Dale feel a wave of tenderness wash over him so strong, him wanted to stroke the thin stately neck in front him, and run his fingers in between and around the sharp edges of his shoulders, massaging each blade with the lightest of caresses. But instead Dale walk back to the living room, fatigue slowing up his every step, and start to pick up the clothes him did take off and leave on the floor last night.

There was a slight frown on Dale's forehead, wrinkling the smooth surfaces of the crab, as him pick up each article: the stout polka-dot tie, the white long sleeve Arrow shirt, the silver tie-pin. And his eyes: small, round and deep-set did have a pensive look to them. Him couldn't understand Ian's coughing and sudden sleeping. It seem to have started just within the last two or three weeks, inching up on them like that, without warning, without a sign. And it didn't even look as if it intend to let up anytime soon, it just seemed hardeared, persistent.

Ian was the only one of Nevin's old sweetheart Dale ever became friends with. Him couldn't understand why Ian in particular, for plenty of them – some young, some not so young – push open the iron gate outside and walk right upstairs into Nevin's bedroom, not even stopping to say 'Howdy-do, Dale. How things and time?' But him figure maybe it was because him see and hear how Nevin and them other ones just use Ian and not much longer fling him one side like old dish rag. And him feel sorry. For in some small way him don't think him get better treatment from Nevin. Or maybe it was because him see and hear too how Ian's poppy-show friends never around when him need them.

Take for example that time when the soldier man from Up Park Camp broke Ian's ankle, and poor Ian did lay-up in a cast going two full months, and not one of the friends did put out a foot to carry him groceries, cook him a meal or even dust down the cobwebs that take set in his living room. Dale alone did go. Miss Kaysen, Ian's mother, did go too, Dale hear later on. But not to nurse Ian back to life. Not to straighten or ruffle the pillows behind his neck. Not to run the back of her thin sallow hand gently against his jaw to check if him have fever or to ask if him want a glass of water. Only to complain how nothing good can amount from all the bad company Ian keep. Nevin didn't put his foot either. For when Dale ask Nevin if him didn't hear what happen to his old time piece, Nevin only kiss his teeth and say whatever a man sow, him bound to reap it.

Dale did tidy-up and clean Ian's apartment the time, wash his clothes and bring him food, for him take after his mother that way;

3

can't stand to see bad things happen to people. Used to watch her take care of his father's two outside children him did have with the postmistress, and even when the postmistress take down sick, is the mother who used to bathe her and give her cerosee tea to draw the fever.

Dale remember the first time him see Ian. Clovy's Bar the Saturday night. Him didn't expect to run into Nevin, for Nevin not much of a bar man. Him rather quiet evenings, moon-light walks and candle-stick dinners. It was four months into the break-up. Nevin drive his car and Dale take the bus or walk. Even friends separate. Those loyal to Nevin only come over while Dale at school. Nevin say him would continue to pay the school fee since business going well. Dale did stay on grateful, but him move from out the master bedroom into a box-shaped little room at the far end of the house whose narrow rectangular windows look out on to white cobblestones and a railway track no longer in use.

It was still early. Only one or two people on the small dance floor. The rest crowd around the bar or stand up defensively by the pool table, with arms fold loosely across chests. Over head disco lights spin bright and cold. Into the shadows, behind clouds of smoke, Dale sip his drink slowly. Him hug up and kiss the people him know, nod to the rest him not as keen with. Watch the bartender serve drinks and flirt with every other customer. All of a sudden him spot Nevin swaggering up to the bar. Dale's eyes follow the trail of people behind, drink trembling slightly. Him breathe easy again as Nevin alone take a seat at the bar.

Dale watch his profile, light and dark against the revolving lights: the close cut hair and burdensome moustache that cover the top lip and leave the bottom one pucker out. The firm square chin with the dimple at the tip. The scar by his lip in the shape of a centipede adding a sinister look. A familiar softness slide down into Dale's belly. Him wonder if him should go over, ask Nevin to dance. Him like the song them playing now. 'McArthur's Park', Donna Summer. More fill up the dance floor. Somebody bounce him, spill the Pepsi. Him put out his hand in time, the liquid splash to the floor. Dale push his way over to the bar, elbows and hips digging into bony behinds and soft bellies. Sweat fasten the short sleeve yellow shirt on to his back and blotch the underarm.

4

But by the time him catch up to the bar, Nevin was gone. Dale focus on the honey-coloured boy Nevin was dancing with. Tall and slim, about nineteen going on. Face: young, soft-looking, narrow like a peanut. A small black mole kiss his left cheek close by his nose. Body lithe, movements easy, the boy dance around Nevin, hands brushing lightly, playful. The grin come quick to his lips, widening his features, showing short, white teeth with a gap in the middle. Them walk off the floor, the boy fluttering in front, Nevin behind: stout, wide-shouldered, strutting confident, the centipede by his lip subdued.

Dale kiss his teeth and turn away, easing back into the shadows, against the concrete columns. Five years ago Nevin used to strut behind him same way. Buy him plenty clothes and parade him off to every friend at every function. Cause mouths to water, eyes to shine bright. Those days them used to go away together all the time. A weekend up in Montreal. Four or five days in some guest house or other in Trelawny. Back then Nevin used to look in his eyes and tell him things as if Dale alone mattered.

On his way out, Dale stop and look over his shoulder one last time. The two of them were sitting up at the bar around the white formica counter, elbows brushing, eyes fasten, and knees, hitch up to the highest rung on the stool, rubbing against one another.

Them did last four whole weeks. Nevin and the fellow, Ian. While them other ones sprawl out on the couch and cock-up stockinged feet on the coffee table like them own the house, as them wait while Nevin grab a fresh suit of clothes, Ian used to wait outside on the verandah, if him leave from inside Nevin's pale yellow Datsun any atall. And when Dale ask why him don't come inside, him would always shake his head, no, and start to comment on the seven foot morning glory Dale have growing outside, the colourful antimacassars Dale crochet and have spread over the arms and backs of the white plastic chairs on the verandah, and even the straw mat sitting in the doorway Dale weave himself that welcomes them all inside.

One day while the two were standing up outside against the hedge, sipping ice cold lemonade from the pitcher-full Dale made earlier that morning, Dale did suddenly run upstairs and back down again, tired and out of breath, with the bedspreads, tablecloths and cabinet top doilies him used to embroider while his mother was alive. Ian did tell him right away about the design school on Flowers Hill, and how Dale must apply if him interested in sewing. Him, personally, would pick up and drop off the applications tomorrow.

But Dale did only shake his head, eyes thoughtful. 'No more sewing for me. Furthermore, I only have a few terms left before I get the Geography degree. Might as well just finish up. Nevin spending so much already . . .'

But Ian only fling the remainder of Dale's sentence one side and continue on: 'You might even branch out into fashion design,' Ian express to him, hands and fingers fluttering. 'Bigger money than that you can't find. But them have other things too. Fashion retail, the line of business Nevin and his mother into, arts and crafts. You can teach it if you like that.'

Ian did go on to reel off a whole long list of things Dale could do with his life, before Nevin came back and grunt out to Ian that him was ready to leave. Maybe them can finish the conversation another time.

Nevin didn't seem to mind the friendship at first. Maybe it looked to him as if Dale was finally accepting that them mash-up for good. But after him see how Ian get his own set of keys, how him sleep over on the couch downstairs in the living room some nights, even prepare dinner now and again and wash-up the dishes, all of a sudden Dale notice that every time Nevin come home and see Ian, a scowl seem to always envelop his face, and not long after his entire body.

One evening after dinner finish and dishes put away, Nevin and Dale retire to the living room as usual. Perch-up on the orange-and-white hassock in front the small colour television, Dale watch the 7.30 news, while across from him in the light blue couch them pick out together, Nevin cut up dry tobacco for his pipe, the blade of the knife tapping dully against the cardboard cover of a book. The clock on the wall, next to the batik Dale bring from Haiti, several vacations back, tick round slowly and without much sound.

Then Dale hear Nevin kiss his teeth, and when him turn around to look, Nevin was kneeling down on the floor, pulling out a pair of black, pointed-toe shoes with silver round the mouths from underneath the couch. And after what seem like a heavy sigh and a long pause, him ask Dale: 'How come Ian's shoes still here?' Then him fling the pair of shoes one side and start to pace around the room, tea-coloured hands clenched behind, a crease lining his forehead, the centipede throbbing violently. 'How come Ian won't sleep at his own yard when night come down?'

Dale sigh out loud and continue to watch the programme. Him didn't see the point in answering. Granted, it wasn't his house. Him don't pay rent either. But for all the hours and overtime him put in, his friends have a right to come and go as them please. Not so much sweetheart. For that is another story altogether. But his friends must be comfortable.

'How come him always here?' Nevin bawl out, hovering behind the hassock. 'How come we just can't spend evenings alone together anymore? Sometimes I just want to come home to a little peace and quiet, but no. Him always here talking about one fellow or another him have a crush on. Always playing the music loud and showing off a new dance step. Always showing off some new pants him buy, or sew or borrow.'

Nevin pause. Dale could feel the glare in his neck-back. The room starting to feel warm as if no air was coming in through the half-open shutters.

'Dale,' Nevin cry out, voice thinning, 'you not listening to me?'

'Ian is me friend,' Dale give out softly and firm, eyes turn to the television same way, the crab on his forehead glistening in the heat, his back stiff and straight. For him didn't understand the exact root of Nevin's jealousy. If it stem from Dale's friendship with Ian or Ian's friendship with Dale.

The following week Dale pick up an extra toothbrush from Red Hills Pharmacy and put it next to the other two in the little pink cup.

Dale didn't concern himself with Ian for the remainder of that weekend. Sundays were usually full days, and him often needed all of Saturday to prepare and half if not all of Monday to recuperate. Sunday mornings from 8 to 10.15, him teach three sections of Sunday School at The Gospel According To St Luke's Episcopal Church, where solemn-eye Madonnas clutching baby Jesus stain each window, and on any given Sunday morning, its narrow pews could fit anywhere from five to seven hundred people.

Dale had been teaching there going five years now, ever since him move in with Nevin. The very first Sunday morning him did set off, bright and early, to the bus stop up the road, him was more than surprised to find out that Nevin's mother, Mrs Morgan, who live on the other side of the house with Nevin's older sister Rose and invalid father, play the pipe organ there every third Sunday of the month. It was always a joy to sit down and watch Mrs Morgan, her face full of lines like old lace, as she proudly take her seat on the stool close to the organ, situate her handbag firmly by her high-heeled black pumps, arrange the pleats of her dress over wide knee-caps, square-up her shoulders and proceed to run ringed fingers deftly over the keyboard bleeding out notes that ripple off the keys, dance in the air, fill every crevice, every crack throughout the building leaving the entire congregation rapt with awe.

She drag Dale along with her to every harvest, every nine night, to the bedside of every ailing sick. She introduce him to all and sundry down at the church (except for a slight and ashen-faced woman, who'd arrive late every Sunday that she attend, dressed from head to toe in black as if perpetually mourning the loss of something or somebody taken away from as far back as childhood. Then the woman would take a seat noiselessly at the far back of the church away from the prying stares of the congregation and after service would never linger with other women to discuss the quality of the preaching, the age of the wine served at communion, the lack of creases in Mr Samuel's plaid trousers, or the fact that Miss Irene already wore that same red frock to church last week and to prayer meeting the week before. After service, she'd promptly pick up her white purse with black sequins lying by her side, toss her head to the sky and walk straight-back out the church, the heels of her shoes noiseless on the thick red rug.) And before long, the entire congregation came to know Dale as Brother Singleton, showering on his shoulders the same amount of respect reserved only for esteemed members. Deacon Roache, own self, would sometimes call upon Dale to lead prayers, conduct baptisms, fill in at weddings, communions, burials.

Sometimes after service Dale would follow the older women into the kitchen at the back of the church where the wide back windows look out on to the well-kept garden and neatly arranged flowers and help them rinse out the communion dishes and wine-soiled tablecloths. And at that time, them would pinch his round cheeks and ask how come a nice-looking fellow like him not married yet. Miss Pearle, especially, a tall heavy woman with silver hair, who sing soprano, and have several pertinent teeth missing, would always smile down at Dale, her breath stale and rancid, and remind him of her two lovely daughters she just dying to get off her hands. And Dale would smile down into the collar of his jacket, the blood rushing to his cheeks all of a sudden, the crab quivering nervously, and tell them him wasn't ready to be tied down yet. Him still want more time to spread his oats. And all five of them would laugh, heavy throaty laughs that rumble inside the room, tumbling blindly against the walls and floorboards, frightened by Dale's honesty, not exactly understanding what him mean, but loving him even more for the confusion and perplexity.

At 2 o'clock, Dale would slip home and prepare dinner for Nevin, who'd probably spend the entire morning lying up in bed with the window open and a warm breeze bathing his jaw, ruffling the blond fuzz on the centipede, as him comb every corner of the Sunday papers, pausing now and again to relight his pipe and sip from the glass of brandy perched on the head of his bed. Sometimes if lucky and time permit, Dale nap for half hour before leading Bible Study 4.30 to 6, and then Young People's Meeting 7.30 to 10. Young People's Meeting was his favourite. For it was here that the late-teenage members of the congregation would seek private counselling. Here Dale could listen to the smooth rise and fall of his own reassuring voice as it wash over the grief-stricken face and head of some youngster who was impregnated by her godfather, or whose father was dying from cancer, or whose uncle was recently imprisoned, or whose parents were splitting up, or who was being molested by his grandfather, or who couldn't understand why him was still looking at other boys even though him

9

was baptised. And to this youngster in particular, Dale would repeat the very same words Pastor Bowles had said to him, Dale, ten years back, in the basement of the Pentecostal church him and his mother used to attend for twelve straight years.

'Son,' and the English man did take Dale's limp young hands into his cracked and hardened ones, the sightless eyes behind the foggy lens of his dark glasses staring fixedly to the right of Dale's left shoulder, 'it is not for us to question the doings of the Almighty.' His face was tangerine-coloured, smooth, almost ageless, and without hairs. His thin lips tremble as him speak, nostrils of his beak widening, narrowing, false teeth clapping click-clack like the hooves of a horse on concrete. 'It is for us to accept, son, to accept and bear persecution. To accept and bear the humility, the stonings, the insults, the loneliness. Not to question. For it is the will of the Almighty. We are just vessels on this sea of life . . .'

Dale had run almost tumbling from the dark oppressiveness of the room into the peaceful green of the sunny churchyard, exhilarated, reassured, suddenly ennobled by the vastness of the cross him alone must bear on his slim feeble back. Sitting quiet on a stone bench in the middle of the churchyard under the almond tree, chubby legs swinging aimlessly, the green jacket of his suit folded neatly beside him, white shirt open at the throat, tie stuffed recklessly into his trouser pocket, him'd resolve then to bear it majestically, to turn the other cheek when the sharp edge of the stone clapped against his head, when the steel-toed tips of police shoes elbow him in the sides, when his friends pile ridicule upon ridicule on his curved shoulders.

And this is what Dale would tell that particular youngster who would come, his young face as soft as melted chocolate, suffused with shame and dread. For Dale knew that if the youngster had gone anywhere else, them would probably tell him he'd obviously been born in sin, why continue to live in it? Why not cleanse himself of this sin rightaway so there would be a place for him close to God? And the purgation would follow quickly with Deacon Roache in the lead, and there'd be endless prayer meetings, endless consultations, endless accumulations of shame and guilt on the part of the youngster. And in the end, maybe that youngster would gird his waist, fasten his eyes tight and choose a Sister, but then maybe him would ease his soul and continue to live with the sin gnawing ferociously at the base of his throat morning, noon and night.

In front the house that Dale share with Nevin, right next to the verandah was a small plot of land. While most people on his street plant grass on it, then water it each evening and call it lawn, Dale turns theirs into farm land. And so those evenings when him and Nevin quarrel, when the house too hot-hot and oppressive, or when him just want to air his head from his studies, him would come outside with his hoe, shovel and paring knife. And when him don't clear the land and mulch it, weed the grass and plough it, him sprinkle carrot and tomato seeds into rows and plant yam and cocoa beside them. But other times him just run his toes in the soil and think about things.

Sometimes him think about University and the courses him was taking toward his Geography degree. At first it was going to be business school so him and his mother could operate the crafts shop together. But after she pass, the desire to embroider and weave simply picked up itself and left as well. The memory of the two of them sitting quiet in the kitchen, she in the rocker by the oil stove in the corner, him on a hard bench leaned against the wall, hunched over yards and yards of wool, haunted him often. Her disease was far gone by then. She couldn't pursue a conversation for long anymore. She couldn't even be trusted to follow a specific path for a short distance for she would end up elsewhere. She couldn't follow the lines of a pattern for a dress with a pair of scissors. All she could do was embroider. And she would sit for hours and hours, humming to herself while she compose the most intricate and detailed of designs, her glossy brown eyes pierced to the rounded tips of the white needles, pausing now and again to sip slowly from a glass of water on a small table to her left, to answer a question Dale had put to her several hours back, to carry on a conversation that had started the day before yesterday.

It was Nevin who suggested the teaching degree after noticing how Dale would spend hours and hours on a Saturday night enraptured in his preparation for Sunday School and Bible Study

11

and how much him would be brimming with stories of his pupils on his return home. And it wasn't that Dale did have a long-standing passion for the study of the earth's surface, its features, the effects of human activities and whatever else Geography entails, why him went ahead and not only followed Nevin's advice to choose this particular course of study, but there was something discerning about the pear-shaped face and wrinkled throat of the old white-haired English woman who teach the course.

And at first him thought that maybe it was just her method of teaching, for she made learning so simple that him was often surprised at how easily him could excel in her class, but after enrolling in her lectures several more times, him come to realise that it was because of certain peculiarities she would exhibit. For example, in the middle of a lecture, in the middle of a multi-syllabled word she would all of a sudden just stop. And for a full three minutes, she'd run her tongue slowly and carefully over the smooth surfaces of her gums, maybe even lingering for a while inside the darkened cavity of a tooth, prodding at the uneven edges, the soft abscessed root, before picking up the final syllable and continuing on. Other times, it was the particular way she would laugh, after giving her own dry lifeless joke, that sounded so much like angels singing in a choir accompanied by the enchanted chimes of an old-fashioned harp. She reminded Dale of his mother.

Sometimes while digging away at the soil, Dale think too about his younger sister abroad and the police man she live with, dreams him have each night and what them mean. Other times him think about Nevin and his family. Rose, Nevin's older sister, must be pregnant again, him figure, for she tell him 'howdy' two evenings in a row and has been laughing going on two whole months straight. Usually she don't laugh atall. For whenever the little caterpillar-shaped blood clot inside her womb slip out, as she get up to pass water in the early hours of the morning, she take to her bed weeks and months at a time, her face shadowed with pain. And nothing atall can pass through her mouth. Not hollering. Not food. Not even a word to her Rastafarian man, Barry.

Dale think too about Nevin's father, Mr Morgan. Five years now, him and Nevin been living at the house together, and Dale still can't tell if Mr Morgan's voice is low or if it is high. If him talk intelligently atall about things or if him ramble on, one nonsense after another. According to what Nevin did tell him, the one and only time Mr Morgan came home drunk and raise his voice and hand to Mrs Morgan, in them forty years together, she did chuck him down the stairs. 'We stand up and watch as him roll down one step and then the other,' Nevin did tell Dale the Sunday, 'fingers too weak and numb from the rum drinking to fasten on to anything.' His voice did sound far off like him was outside, not next to Dale around the kitchen table. 'Mama and Rose start up the bawling. But my mouth just open wide. Not a sound could pass through. Not till him reach the bottom. Then I call for help.'

Dale couldn't say a word at first. All along him used to think Mr Morgan was just mean and bad-tempered. For every time Dale would tell him howdy, the old man just kiss his teeth and wheel off in his chair, his back curved. Him used to think maybe Mr Morgan just didn't like the lifestyle him and Nevin lead, even though Mrs Morgan don't say anything atall about it. 'What the police say?' Dale did finally ask him, feeling sorry for the fleshy-necked man all of a sudden.

'Nothing, really.' Nevin shift round in his chair and push away the plate from in front him. Darkness shadowed his two eyes. 'That him spine crack. Probably won't walk again. But barring that, them don't like interfere in domestic affair.'

Dale remember how Nevin didn't say much after that. In fact, him didn't even bother to finish the fish dinner. Him get up from around the table and went upstairs. Not long after, him put on pyjamas and crawl under the sheet. Them didn't touch atall that night.

Ian was over again the following week. That afternoon, Dale was sitting in the swivel chair in the room him take over as study. Him'd repaint it himself off-white with peach trimmings, and it was big and wide and full of plenty sunshine along with just the faintest smell of burning incense. Through mail order, him did send away to England for the lace peach curtains that match

13

perfect with a pastel but floral couch from country. It was in here, spot with hibiscus, croton, chrysanthemums and ferns, where him keep in an oak bookcase and on wooden shelves evenly aligned against the wall, books from high school and the ones him was using now up at the University, in addition to other solemn-looking volumes of classics bound in dark cloth his mother received one by one each month for two years from a subscription to a place based in England; the scrapbook with the poems him set down now and again; subscription to National Geographic; clothes and the folder with newspaper clippings of extraneous happenings. Whenever it wasn't a story about the faceless baby born to the nine-year-old girl up at Spauldings General, it was one about the stoning to death of the University professor due to his immoral acts with young calves.

The black schoolteacher desk with faded etchings of: 'Jesus Saves', 'Batty-man' and 'One Love Jamaica' sat near two large glass windows that overlook, from one side, the green-skin mango tree outside, and the way its branches, thick and crooked, cast themselves confidently into Mrs Morgan's backyard; the row of houses on his street that all looked the same; across Red Hills Road where higglers line both sides selling over-ripe june plums, roast corn and sky juice; and way up into Stony Hill where all the houses have swimming pools around the back and the winding driveway leading up to the verandahs have pruned weeping willows on either sides. Pasted along the painted white walls were religious quotations taken from 'The Lord's Prayer', Psalm 100 and Psalm 23, outlined in a very elaborate and gothic lettering that had taken him days upon days to accomplish.

The other window look out on the large expanse of red dirt – the play field belonging to Villa Road All Age School, the stained glass windows of St Luke's, Crew Corner bus stop and the parking lot of Exodus Gallery and Mall. Arranged on his desk, in meticulous order, in a specially made hand-carved wooden frame (baptism gift from his godfather), varying by colour, type and print size was his collection of fountain pens. Forty-eight in all. Pass the bathroom, down the hall and around the corner was where him sleep when night come down. Back around that way, him couldn't hear who was coming and going and from which room.

14

Dale was sitting at the desk, the Geography text for his class open wide in front him. It was about two or three the afternoon. Outside schoolchildren shriek loud and laugh heavy as them romp and kick pebbles on the way home. The door handle downstairs rattle and turn, and before Dale could make it downstairs, Ian appeared in the doorway.

'Ian Kaysen!'

'Ah, Dale Singleton.' Ian glide up the stairs, shoes whispering against the carpet, long, slender fingers caressing the banister.

'You didn't go to work?' Dale seat himself back round the desk.

'Yes,' Ian nod, as him finger the combination on the briefcase and take out the golden cigarette case, the lawyer man, Bill, buy him the last birthday.

Dale wait till him take the first three puffs, find a hanger for his jacket and ease himself on to the couch. Him learn from practice that nothing atall budge from Ian's lips till him comfortable.

'I take half day. Tired of the blasted hot office, balance sheet and tax statements.' Him cross his legs, tilt head backwards and blow the smoke to the ceiling, lips slightly pouted. Manicured fingernails stretch taut against the shoulder of the couch. 'Me go downtown. You know me, always looking for what I don't put down.'

'Anything good.'

Ian pause for a while, eyes far off. The light dusting of face powder soak up all speckles of sweat, leaving his face cool and calm. 'You know how it is with the upcoming election.'

Dale shake his head. 'I can't wait for it to be over. For now you have to be extra careful who you talk to, what you say, the colour clothes you wear. You hear on the radio this morning how them shoot this poor man on his way to work for wearing a red shirt? The gunman assume him was a member of the National Party.'

Ian shake his head. 'Yesterday, it take me almost three hours to reach home from the office. Everyone of the major roads block-off with old car and burning tyre and oil drums. I just hope them don't bother with the curfews again like last election. Police just slap-slap you with batons as them have a mind. Anyway, bad news aside, I see the loveliest man at the bus stop, though.' Ian's face break down into a grin, eyes deep, mysterious.

'Oh yeah?' Dale ease back in his chair, arms folded behind his head.

Ian stop and shudder, voice husky, heavy with emotions. 'Big shoulders, face coarse and rough-looking. Just the way I love them.' Him inhale more of his cigarette and exhale slowly, lips tunnel-shaped. 'I was walking past, but I couldn't help meself. I had to stop.' Him get up from off the couch and walk towards the window, brushing imaginary balls of dust off grey pin-striped trousers that flow from his narrow hips like a gown. Him loosen the cuff links of his silk shirt, drop them in his pocket and turn up the sleeves, revealing thin hairy arms.

'Mechanic or something. You can tell. Stink of car oil. Tractor-trailer boots that drag, for him don't lace them up. Finger nails bite-up bite-up and dirty. Cap turn backwards. Shirt wide open, and not a single solitary hair on that man's chest.' Ian sigh loud, voice distance. 'Smooth just like baby's skin. You could see the waist of the white underpants before it sink inside the tear-up dungarees.

'So of course, I had to take a seat next to him.' Ian bat his eyes, pause, take a deep breath, make sure his nostrils flare, spit on his finger then bend down and rub dirt from off the tip of his black shoes and continue on.

Dale watch from across the room, a grin flirting with the edges of his mouth.

'So I put on my best man walk. You know . . .' Ian thrust his fists inside the pants pockets and start to strut around the room, each foot step heavy. 'And prop up myself next to him.' Ian sit back down in the couch, legs open wide, right hand gripping his crotch.

Dale start to laugh.

'Don't laugh. It's a serious thing. That's what you have to do to get them attention. Act just like them. None of this prim and proper business. Them would never even stop to glance at you. And in my deepest man's voice, I ask him which horse was winning at Kymanis Park today. For that's what them do with them money. Pay child's support and gamble the rest. But him wasn't friendly atall.' Ian's face take on a gloominess, as him

16

resume a more comfortable pose back on the couch. 'Just mumble out Shining Star or something or other.'

'What you know about horse racing, anyway? Suppose him did start to engage you?'

'Me love, you have to grab the horse by the collar. Can't wait around and wonder if and but. I figure maybe him smoke. So I put the briefcase on my lap and start to unlock it. Lo and behold, my tube of Vaseline intensive care was sitting right on top.'

'Serve you damn right,' Dale burst out, voice agitated, laughter gurgling in his throat. 'You think him see it?'

'Of course, him see it. Those lovely beady eyes wouldn't miss a thing. I mumble something about sunburn, or cold sore, I can't quite remember which, but lucky thing the bus pull up and him board it.'

Dale shake his head, smiling. 'I can't understand what you find in them, you know. Bill look after you well, but that don't satisfy you. You want the tough, ugly, ignorant man who more than quick to call you names and burst up your head.'

'But if him nice looking, what I must do?' Ian grin. 'I see some lovely colour TV downtown on sale too. I want to buy one for my mother, for Mother's Day. What you think?'

The grin slide off Dale's face and harden the lines around his mouth. Him didn't say anything. Him take his eyes off Ian and lodge them somewhere over his head top. And from the wings them catch sight of a spider building a nest in one corner of the wall.

'Decent sale, too,' Ian continue on, voice raising-up with excitement. 'Thirty and forty per cent off. I know that she would like that. She could give away the old one she have now. For as you cough, that thing break down. She could set it down next to the organ and maybe put one or two figurines on top . . .'

Still, Dale didn't say anything. Ian's two eyes did take on a gloss him never see before, as him sprawl back in the couch, legs cross over one another, shirt unbuttoned halfway down for it was a warm afternoon. Dale wonder if Ian didn't remember how the mother send back the silk frock him buy last Christmas. The one him save up two whole months for. How she not even did open

17

the box, for when it came back, the wrapping paper didn't even have a scratch, not even a crinkle.

'What size you think I should get, Dale? One of the big ones that sit down on the floor or the normal size ones?'

But him didn't even wait for Dale's answer. Him continue on.

'I know she would like the big one. My mother likes things big and ostentatious. And I am just like her.'

'You think that's the right thing?' Dale ask him quietly, face stern, shiny from the heat outside. Him did only have on shorts and a pair of push-toe slippers. Beads of sweat start to gather up on his wide chest. Dale wasn't a hairy man. And even the little that grow on his head was thinning out quick-and-brisk. Now and again, as him feel the sweat starting to trickle down towards his navel, him use the back of his hand to wipe it dry.

'Because she send back the frock, Christmas?'

Dale didn't answer. Him could see the light fading from Ian's face, and his shoulders that did raise up a little, starting to melt back down into his belly.

'That's because she have one just like it.'

'But what about graduation, Ian?' Dale try to calm his voice, but him could hear it rising. 'Is not everyday you graduate from University? On top of that, she the first person you send invitation. You did even have seat reserve up front for her. And still she didn't show her foot.'

Ian pause before him answer. 'She say she couldn't find the invitation. Say she did put it on the dresser in her room. But my sister, with her touch-touch self, probably moved it when she was cleaning. She say she really wanted to come . . .'

From over where him sit down around the desk, legs stretch out in front and fold at the ankles, Dale wanted to reach over and hold Ian. Put Ian's head next to his chest and just hold it right there against his heart. But him didn't move. That was one cross him couldn't help Ian carry. Other things him would interfere in, but not family. Blood thicker than water his mother used to say. Instead him watch Ian sink down lower into the couch.

The room did take on a sudden glumness. Dale get up from the desk and walk towards the window. Him push it open. The warm air from outside brush against his face. Him inhale it. The

18

laughing from outside draw his attention. It was a raucous horse laugh, ringing loud amidst the noise of Red Hills Road traffic; the kind of a laugh a woman give out when the man she with tell her which position him enjoy most last night, or about which river basin him would swim across and which mountain top him would climb over just to find her if she ever left him.

Outside the window, Dale could see Rose picking up clothes from off the line that run from one branch of the mango tree to the electric light post. Him couldn't see her face, her steel-rod back was to him, but now and again she would take the clothes pin prop between her lips and fling it to the side of her where Barry, the long-haired Rastafarian man, she have two miscarriages for, was sitting down on a piece of dry wood peeling a grapefruit. Back in the room, Dale hear the matches strike as Ian light-up another cigarette. Him listen to the shoes clip-clop as him get up walk downstairs.

As far as Dale could see, Ian shouldn't've said a word to Miss Kaysen about the lawyer man, Bill. No matter how much him love the mother and want to tell her things. For him could tell right off, from all him hear about her, that when she take away her loving, she didn't plan to give it back next week. Now and again, she attend services at St Luke's. His own eyes had never blessed her, or not that him know of, but from what him gather, people never glad to see her. Them say she love to find fault and keep malice. Can hold grudge longer than anybody them know. Love to cause contention. Them claim that her contribution to the collection plate was always next to nothing. That she never have a welcoming smile to offer anyone, only several hard lines that crease her mouth corners and a hard gleam in her eyes.

But Ian love his mother to distraction. Not so much the father. Not when him was alive or even now since him pass on, going thirteen months. Ian have eyes only for the mother. From every paycheque, each month, a portion always send off registered mail to the mother. On top of that, she get hat and crockery every Easter, jewellery Independence time, and a one-week paid vacation to Miami every birthday. But sometimes when a thing make you happy, you don't feel good just keeping it to yourself. You want everybody to know. You want them face to widen out with glee, them eyes brim over with merriment, them belly shake with excitement same way your own. Well, Miss Kaysen didn't have any merriment left in her heart when she find out Easter gone, the lawyer she used to hear so much about, was starting to court Ian.

Nevin did tell Dale the story. For it started around the time Nevin and Ian were just starting to know each other. It was Miss Kaysen's birthday. Enclosed in the same gift-wrapped box with the snow-white silk evening dress, pearl earrings and matching necklace sent certified mail, was a type-written letter to the mother explaining the state of his heart where men were concerned.

Two days later when Nevin arrive 7.00 sharp at Ian's apartment to feast upon the four-course, candle-light meal Ian plan was to prepare, him find Ian seated, back hunched over, on the emerald green rug in the middle of the living room, dress-up from head to toe in his mother's white silk frock, earrings clip to the lobes of his pinna, necklace tumbling down his hardened chest-plate. Him was whimpering softly, thumb and forefinger tenderly caressing ashes from a small white envelope that had his name scrawled on with a piece of charcoal. It was the letter the mother burn to cinders and send back.

That same evening, Ian beg Nevin please to drop him by the mother's house. Him have to talk to her desperately.

'You sure, Ian?' Nevin did ask, not really wanting to drive all the way over to Spanish Town Road. 'I mean it look as if she mad as hell with you. I mean, look.' Nevin stretch out his hands, empty, at the envelope with the ashes.

'You dropping me or not?'

And Nevin did have to put on back his heavy black cloak, for it was raining like hell outside, first rain storm in over two months, and drive the forty-eight minutes to the mother's house in silence, Ian's hands, cold with fear, locked tight inside his.

Nevin say him waited outside in the car, watching from the window cloudy with steam while Ian scale the gate, chain-up with a steel padlock. On the verandah, Ian fumble in his pocket for the house key to the front door. Him slip it inside the lock and turn one way, then another. Nevin say him could sense the frustration just by looking at his shoulders, the way them sag heavy like laden

20

crocus bags around him. Then all of a sudden, Ian start to pound on the solid wooden door with his fist, hollering out 'Mama' on top of his voice, for it was raining and with the water hitting hard against the galvanised zinc roofs and dropping clamorous inside the gutters by the side of the house, and then making its way boisterous into corrugated steel drums that collect water for the chickens around the back, she probably couldn't hear him, especially if she have wads of cotton stuff-up in the holes of her ears to keep out the sounds of evil.

Finally the door open up with such force that it pull Ian headlong inside. Fifteen, twenty minutes passed. And still Ian didn't come back. Inside the car, the heat grow insufferably. Finally Nevin say him put on back the cloak and leap out the car, dancing his way over puddles of water that settle themselves all over the road, and scale the gate into her yard. The rain was beating down mercilessly on her rose bush whose baby shoots were just starting to sprout. The verandah door was locked, but one of the wooden louvres was half open, so Nevin prise it wider with a piece of stick that Miss Kaysen had mounted to the vine of a spider plant, probably to help it spread.

According to Nevin the living room was in complete darkness. Him could spot only the silver tips of Ian's shoes and the white paws of a cat or young puppy walking around in circles by his feet, but that was all.

'But why you have to change the lock, Mama? Why you have to send back . . .'

'I am not your mother.'

Nevin say him jump back from the window, for her voice was so close, almost as if she was speaking right behind him, right in his neck.

'I don't know who you are. So please go.'

'But, Mama.'

'Don't come back. Go. Go now.'

The tips of the shoes jumping backwards as if she was chucking him in the chest.

'Mama, you just can't disown me so. You just can't . . .'

'I never did like you from the beginning. Miss Iris couldn't get you out. Twist up yourself inside me womb like you plan was to

21

stay. Them did have to force cow-itch tea down me throat to get you to budge. Even then you were no damn good. Should've followed me heart and put a blasted end to you, then.'

Nevin say him couldn't listen anymore. Him close the window and walk back to the car. Him wait several minutes, then slowly pull away from the kerb, circling the square several times before driving back to the house to pick up Ian who was walking in the middle of the road towards the lighted eyes of the car, head bent, shoulders drooped, hands deep inside his pockets, the rain pouring off his tall, slender frame, for the mother refuse to lend him a piece of plastic to throw over his head so him wouldn't catch a cold.

As Dale continue to think about Ian and Miss Kaysen, all of a sudden his nose started to sweat. It was the retching and heavy wheezing him hear first. Him wanted to cover his ears, block out the sound, but Ian call out his name same time, and him rush out the room and down the stairs two at a time, heart thumping out loud. Him didn't want to look to see how Ian's eyes had turned red, or how the foam, white and thick, would have curdled at the edges of his moustache. Instead him run pass the figure doubled-over on the couch, hands press against chest, the cigarette burning by the winged-tip shoes, and into the kitchen for the roll of paper towel on the counter to wipe-up the phlegm Ian was spitting out. One after the other. Some brown. Purple. Others pinkish.

Late February 1978

'I have to carry Ian to doctor,' Dale tell Nevin one evening. Him was sitting at the foot of Nevin's bed, his two hands holding up his jaw.

'Ian can't carry himself to doctor?' Nevin grunt out from behind the L'Amour Western. Him did have the entire collection line-up on the cinder-block-and-board bookshelf against the wall. 'You is him caretaker?'

Dale feel the anger rise-up to his chest. Him swallow it back down. Determined not to rise to the bait tonight. With his big toe him play with the foot of sock roll-up on the floor. 'The whole heap of cough-cough getting from bad to worst. The other day him vomit blood. I don't think him eating. Him look meagre-meagre to me, bad.'

Nevin rest the book on his lap, back lean-up against the bedhead. Turn the leaves one or two times, stroke the few strands of beard that were starting to grow on his chin. Adjust his glasses firmly on his nose. 'It catching?'

Dale sigh out loud. Him raise his head to look at Nevin and then turn away. Him used to like the scar that run alongside Nevin's mouth corner. Dog-bite from when him was small. The ridges and grooves as his forefinger crawl over it used to calm and relax him. But not of late. In fact not much about Nevin engage him of late. Not the smile that crinkle his eyes and flare out his nose. Nor the coarseness of his cheek from each day-old beard. The room was empty now. Dale did pack it up. It didn't have the little green rug Dale did sew himself that used to sit at the bedside, nor the reading lamp next to the bedhead. The space on the wall

23

where the picture used to hang, the one with Dale and his mother framed, in front the big Ackee tree, look white and bare.

'Since you not coughing up blood, I don't suppose so.' Dale's voice did have a chill to it. 'Considering how you always up inside everybody.'

The silence last one full second.

'You expect me to live like a damn nun,' Nevin holler out, voice gaining in momentum, the centipede raised, starting to bristle. 'You expect me to walk with my head hang down. Not talk to anybody. Not look at people.'

Dale could feel the headache coming on, the one that always spread crossway his forehead and pulsate by his temples when them quarrel.

'You expect me to just lie down sleep by meself when night come. After you gone to your room and bolt the door behind you. And it wasn't me who started it. It was you who wanted the relationship to be open. You complain that you too young to stay settle. You want to see other people. Even before it could settle good, you bring this married man into me house, into me bed.'

Dale suck his teeth, brows starting to furrow-up, disturbing the smooth surfaces of the crab. 'Go on. Blame me. Every damn thing happen is me who cause it. Alexander Pilot didn't cause anything. You know it wasn't working . . .'

'Wasn't working out, my tail.' Nevin fling the book across the room and roll out the bed. Him walk towards Dale and jerk his face upwards. 'Is you mash we up,' him scream in Dale's face. 'You and that shit house, Alexander, who don't even respect his wife and children. What kind of man is that?'

Dale could feel Nevin's breath, hot on his face. It was coming out short and quick, and his chest, broad and naked, heaved up and down. His eyes were wild, unfocused, his wide nostrils quivered like those of a horse. The veins on his forehead swelled out vigorously on his forehead. Dale wonder if Nevin was going to strike him. Grab his head and ram it against the wall. Like the time him come home sudden and find Alexander. Cause twelve stitches across the middle of Dale's forehead and a circular scar that raise up now and again in the shape of a crab when it has a mind. Dale hold his breath, body tense. Him did have his things ready in the other room. If Nevin lick him one more time, that was it. Only his mother had the right to manhandle him that way. Not lover. Not sweetheart.

But even before Dale could finish think the sentence, even before him could register the slight movement, him hear the whizzing and did only have time to duck down, before the glass crash against the wall, and the alarm clock scatter to the floor, its belly open-up wide, contents spread out. The room stay silent after that. Even Red Hills Road seem quiet. Now and again a motor-bike roar pass, or a bus screech out loud as it stop sudden. Just below, Mr Morgan mutter to himself and the wheels of his chair rumble as him spin it round and round.

Dale squeeze back the eye water burning behind his nose. Feel the throbbing by his temples, the rushing in his head, the dull tremor of the crab. Him think about the little savings him have. The last few months him been dipping into it. Have enough to pay maybe six months' worth of rent, but then what about school fee, and clothes, medical emergencies? Him couldn't face the thought of going back to live with his Aunt Daisy and Mr Rattler, her husband. For even though they treated him kindly, him would always get the feeling that she read his diary when him wasn't there and search through his clothes. Silently Dale get up off the bed and haul on the slippers him did kick to one side. Through his right eye corner him could see Nevin stand-up alongside the window, hands bury deep inside the trousers pocket, hugging thighs. But him didn't feel like going over to him. Usually after each fight, him try to talk. Express where him think him go wrong, areas that need work. Try and get Nevin to talk about the anger pile-up inside, the frustrations around them love life. But him didn't feel like playing counsellor tonight. Dale tread his way careful pass the splinters and continue on downstairs out on to the verandah.

To one side of the plot of land was a thicket of wild thorny roses that Mrs Morgan planted to separate her garden from theirs. The perfume filled the night and from the glare of the nearby street lamp Dale could make out fiery buds just beginning to open. Dale fish out the penknife him always keep in his back pocket and begin to cut the stiff stems crowded with thorns. Maybe him would cut

25

bouquets for the house, one in each room, a vase of Mrs Morgan's half-awake roses to brighten the house, bring back some of the happiness to the relationship.

But just as sudden as it came, the desire flitted away, and Dale drop the penknife and several stems of roses to the ground. Him fall down with them noiseless, on the cool thin dirt, sighing out loud. Him was tired of trying. Tired of holding things together. Tired of fighting. The sky was cloudy, the air still and warm. Crickets and night bugs chirped from somewhere close. Dale's mind run on Alexander Pilot and a calmness engulf him. It loosen the knots from inside his stomach and lift the heavy weight from off his back. Dale think about the first time they met. The Sunday. Alexander did drop off his two little boys at Sunday School. Dale introduced himself. Him remember the handshake. Sturdy but warm. Almost as if it wanted to say something else. Them did talk. Just howdy-do at first. One or two comments about the rise in gas prices, the cold front blowing down from Canada, the building of the new athletic facility at Jose Marti Primary School.

But as more Sundays pass, Dale remember how him used to take more and more notice of this man, especially his eyes. And it wasn't that Alexander did have that special flavour him look for in a man. The sweet talking and compliments him could listen to from now till tomorrow morning. The broad shoulders and heavy chest that could pin him against the fridge or knead him down on the warm linoleum, cause him to grunt out loud. Alexander wasn't particularly generous with flattery, him was a very practical man. And him wasn't shaped smoothly atall either. His body, round and loose, and well out of form, slosh every which way when him walk. But him was a kind man, very knowledgeable about things, and his two eyes: pale green and narrow, could look way down deep inside and stir-up feelings tuck away safe for years. That used to frighten Dale.

Not that him did have things to hide. Yes, him and Nevin have problems, but it wasn't that the same flutter didn't come to his stomach when Nevin run his fingers crossway his back, down his thighs time and time again. It wasn't that him still didn't dream of growing old with Nevin, travelling with him to distant places, probably even buying several acres of land and raising a child or two together. No, it wasn't that Alexander would supplant Nevin.

But it was as if every time him see Alexander all thoughts of Nevin receded for the time being. Them would talk during the short five-minute intermission between each class, for Alexander wasn't much of a church-going man. And from conversations together, Dale gather that him was born in England but been out here since five years of age, that him turn forty-nine June gone even though him don't look it, that him been married now going on eight years with only two cases of infidelity, that him own the house over in Cherry Gardens and looking to buy another, that his wife is a barrister in the Family Court downtown, and that him is the religious education teacher at Cherry Gardens Technical High.

Even up to this day, as him think about it, Dale didn't see anything strange in the way them became friends. Maybe him was naive, but everything just seemed only natural. At first them would meet for soft-drinks downtown, and Alexander would coach him about the classes him must take up at the University. Not long after, the coaching moved on to lunchtime escapades at art galleries and museums in New Kingston, and long evening walks up at Hope in the botanical gardens. And Dale was excited, for this was somebody outside the close-knit circle of Nevin's friends. Somebody him meet on his own who had interests and a life outside of Clovy's Bar. Somebody him feel a tinge of affection toward, maybe because of the way him was still playful with his sons, would always romp rough with them in the churchyard after Sunday School. For when Dale turned seven, his father stopped playing with him and would only bark commands instead, claiming that 'if you play with puppy dog for too long, one day it would lick your nose in public.'

And so by the time Dale bring Alexander over to Nevin's house the day, Dale did know Alexander's favourite author, film director, music composer and painter. Him did know too, the bank where the Pilots keep money as well as the account number and the end of month balance, the location of Precious House of Beauty where Alexander get his hair cut every last Wednesday of the month,

27

how him like his eggs cook, his favourite brand of bubble bath and the tattoo on the right cheek of his buttocks.

Coming out of the park one evening, Alexander already drive off, Dale spy Ian from across the street and immediately him feel shame, the sting flooding his cheeks, spilling into his neck. For a split second him wonder if him should dodge. Slip inside a shop and order a beer. Duck behind a crowd waiting for the next bus. Pretend.

'Dale Singleton,' Ian bawl out from across the street, arms akimbo, back bent slightly forward, eyebrows raise high up into his hair root.

Dale cross the street quickly over to where Ian was starting to create spectacle. 'Is me friend,' him say to Ian first thing, out of breath, eyes focus somewhere around Ian's middle.

'I can see that,' Ian answer, assuming a more relaxed pose as him pick up his leather box-shaped briefcase with his name engraved on the side in gold, straddled between his legs.

Them walk on side by side, Dale silent, Ian looking on interested. A bus pulled up. Hordes of people leap on. But not everyone could fit. The conductor scream at the people inside, him curse, telling them to go down, go down into the blasted bus. Plenty more room at the back. A man cry out for his toes. Somebody with a seat offer to hold a shrieking baby. Outside the bus the conductor still continue to grumble. Him threaten not to move the bus till people move down into the back so everybody can fit.

'Don't look like your type though. But I suppose that in these days of austerity where things are scarce, that is all you can find.'

'Ian Kaysen, mind your own damn business.'

'I minding it.'

Pause. Another bus pull up. The same threats and curses occur.

'So what him do for a living? How much money him make? Where him live?'

Them walk toward Hi-Lo supermarket, shoulders brushing against people coming and going.

'Him married.'

'Married?' Ian slow down, eyebrows starting to arch upwards into his hair root.

Dale saunter on ahead, chunky-looking in blue jeans and a sleeveless white marina.

'Dale Singleton, please don't walk ahead like I am your damn servant waiting behind you, hand and foot.'

Ian catch up. Shoulder to shoulder again. Ian's half the size of Dale's. 'What you mean married? Holy matrimony, minister, exchange of vows, married ring with real woman married?'

Dale nod, scar beginning to crinkle. 'Have two children. Two little boys.'

'Nevin know?'

Silence.

'Well my love, you know you don't have much rights once wife's involved. Is them who get the property when him drop down dead in you bed. Is them who get to take care of him when him fall down sick . . .'

'Don't lecture me, Ian Kaysen.'

But Ian didn't have any stop to stop. Staring straight ahead, narrow hips rustling in the soft folds of his pleated brown suit, him continue on: 'Too scared to come out, them hide behind wife's frock tail. Breed up the place with plenty children, people think them is real man. While my tail out on the line, them still keep work. What a life. Nice and easy. And you add to it.'

Dale didn't say anything. Him walk on silent, slightly out of breath, as him try to match Ian's wide strides.

April 1978

One morning early, even before the day barely stretch crossway the sky brandishing it a fiery orange, streaks of grey and red, and Nevin wake up, Dale make himself a mug-full of mint tea, sip it slowly by the stove in the kitchen, then slip quietly out the house. Him was hoping to get to the hospital early, for maybe Ian would get attend to sooner. Outside, the air was still nippy. Dew splash the edges of trousers foot, and higglers set up tables and open-up baskets full of fruit all along Red Hills Road. Dale stand up talk to the orange and ripe banana lady with the bright blue tie-head till the number 36 bus pull up and him pay the fare and board it.

Him sit down in the first window seat. Across the aisle to his left, one young girl was breast-feeding her baby. Dale turn away his head. Him couldn't understand why this woman, in her loud green frock, was still feeding the baby even though it look big enough to be eating yam and breadfruit by now. And look at the way she hold it! Next thing you know the baby grow with round back. Dale shake his head. It would hurt his mother to see it. She used to be so particular about how children must raise. Out the window, traffic was just starting to pick up. Several women with signs and placards held high protest the recent lay-offs from the bauxite plant. Political slogans heralding the upcoming election colour every building, even Barclay's Bank was spray painted. Dale could see school-children, chequered uniforms starch stiff and press smooth, squat-down outside the bus stop, the oil in them hair glistening bright against the sunlight.

Ian was waiting out on the verandah on his studio, and without even saying howdy-do, the two of them walk back to the bus stop just around the corner.

'I find a place on Webster Avenue,' Dale tell him proudly.

'You still talking that damn nonsense about moving out of Nevin's house, Dale Singleton.' Ian turn to face him.

Dale look away. Ian's voice did take on a harshness he'd never heard before. Eyes too seem dim, breathing kind of hard, like them been walking far. 'Might as well I stop hoping for miracles. Me and him can't get back, Ian. Everything is quarrel-quarrel and big fight.'

Ian kiss his teeth hard. 'Me love, you live with somebody you bound to have differences of opinion. Is a natural thing.' Him pause, arms akimbo, briefcase swaying from his right wrist. Was planning to go on into work after the check-up.

Dale notice the same shortness of breath, a sort of raspiness to the voice almost like wheezing. A JOS bus was pulling up. Him strain his eyes to see if it was the one them want. One lady brush against him with her beat-up, dulcemeena suitcase. Dale turn around to see if she use it and nasty-up his nice white trousers. Would have to stop and trace her this morning.

'I don't understand why you can't just patch-up things,' Ian continue on. 'The love was there already. Last all of five years.'

'It mash up,' Dale tell him, brushing hands together, voice thick. 'Sometimes we look like lovebird own self. Affectionate and loving, everlasting. But it doesn't last long. One little argument and everything blow out of proportion.'

Ian shake his head. 'It pain me sometimes, when I see how him look at you, eyes so big and brown, soft and sad-looking . . .'

'How come you constantly jump on his side, Ian? How come Nevin's feelings more important than mine?' Dale stop. Halfway Tree bus stop did have smatterings of people dawdling about. Some started to turn round and look.

Ian's voice soften, a hint of tiredness shadowing his face. 'Just that me wish me did have somebody to care me like Nevin care you.' His eyes flutter shut and open-up again. But not as bright. Almost like a cloud of sadness cover them over. 'Someone to give me place to put me head when night come down. Pay me school fee.'

And all of a sudden the tenderness in Ian's voice made Dale frightened, made him confused. Made him think about Ian's

31

mother and the heaviness that had suddenly overshadowed the conversation. 'But, you have Bill?'

'Please me love, please me dear. Bill, who?' Ian didn't even bother to raise his eyes and look over at Dale whose face was starting to puzzle over, but also to relax, for the tone was shifting and the heaviness was beginning to dissipate.

'You mash-up?'

'Might as well.' Ian ease the pressure off one slender foot and place it on to the other. 'I know that man now five months. We travel everywhere together. You name it, him buy it and give me. But I couldn't tell you if that man's navel push out or if it push in. We sleep in the same bed some nights, but whether him hang heavy, or just plain medium, these two eyes yet to behold it. I don't know, Dale Singleton, if that man like to tongue-bath hours at a time, or if him would rather a quiet peck on the cheek now and again.'

Dale squelch the surprise in his voice. 'It take some people longer time to feel comfortable.'

'That I agree with. But five months! One. Two. Three. Four. Five.' Ian stretch out a finger at each count. 'I want my business taken care of right away, me love. That kind of celibate life not for me.' Him fumble around for a cigarette, hands trembling as him light it. Him inhale it long, head lean to one side, eyes slightly closed, chest rising, smoke filling out his two sunken cheeks.

The smell of antiseptic and bad sores slap them faces as them step inside the hospital. Then them walk down the corridor, not a word between the two, through two double doors and around one corner, Dale walking briskly ahead, Ian dragging behind, the black leather briefcase brushing against his side with each step. Already eight people were standing up in line.

'Go sit down, rest yourself,' Dale tell Ian, motioning to the row of wooden benches lean up against the sparkling white wall. 'I will talk to the nurse lady.'

But even before him could clear his throat, even before him could open his mouth to lodge the complaint, Dale hear the bawl out then the commotion behind him as the body hit the floor and the benches skid-way across the dull concrete.

Them admit Ian same time.

'The lungs collapse,' the nurse lady tell Dale, as she put the little cap over Ian's nose and start to pump.

Then them strap him up on the stretcher and wheel him out.

Dale wanted to follow after them. But the nurse tell him no. Ian need intensive care. But she will call him. In the meantime please sit down and keep quiet.

Dale bend down to pick up the briefcase from off the floor littered with thermoses of coffee, tea, this morning scalded cow's milk; bundles and cases tie-up with strings, exposing clean and soiled nappies, bottles of warm milk powder, yesterday's dinner reheated early this morning and wrap-up careful in cellophane. The small group of people that did crowd around join back the line. The rest sit down on the bench, hands wedged between laps, faces heavy.

And as Dale sit down in the waiting room, Ian's briefcase crossway his lap, hands holding up his jaw, him wasn't sure whether to start the bawling or to not bother with it atall. Outside the siren of an ambulance wail out loud. Him hear the commotion down the corridor, and the loud speaker overhead calling for Doctor Cadian to report to room 12B right away.

The eye water burn behind his nose. Up ahead more old people and women with enormous bellies crowd in. Dale feel them eyes, questioning. Him think about Ian inside the room stretch out, white sheet pull up to his chest, silver tubes running in and out each nostril, machines blinking red and green, pointers drawing squiggly lines across grey screens. Him wonder about cigarette smoking, the shortness of breath this morning and the constant coughing. If collapse lungs means operation and long length of time inside the hospital, or just quick-stick patch-up and back to normal. His hands start to shake. Dale wrap them tighter around the briefcase, searching inside his mind for something his mother used to say about collapse lungs. Him buck-up instead on the dream Ian tell him about two weeks ago.

They were downtown the afternoon. Dale and Ian and Bill. Sitting outside on the terrace of New Kingston Hotel overlooking the pool. Bill was a man who love to live well and spend plenty money. No one was inside the pool splash-splashing around, only one or two tourist lay-up around the edges in lounge chairs, pink skins lather-up with lotion.

Bill was leading the conversation as usual. Was a man who feel very much inclined to impart knowledge to everybody him think don't know as much. Ian interrupt several times. Other people spending too much time in the spotlight didn't sit easy with him.

'Dream about my father last night,' Ian tell them. 'First time since him dead and bury. Over a year now.' Ian count the months, fingers and lips moving slightly.

'What happen?' Dale did ask, eager, for Ian don't talk about his father much.

'Kind of peculiar,' him tell them, eyes picking up distance, forehead knit-over. 'Crying as usual. God!' Him shake his head, face suddenly overcast. 'My father always used to cry. Every argument between him and my mother would cause him to fold up himself in the hammock outside on the verandah and holler. Maybe that's why I didn't like him much.' Ian's voice harden. Him drag on the cigarette, eyes squint shut against the smoke, cheeks hollow.

Bill reach over to him, but draw back the minute him notice the waiter hovering around. Him take a sip of the Drambuie and coffee instead. Dale suck-up a mouthful of the orange-flavour aerated water through the straw. Didn't like much the taste of liquor swirling around inside his mouth and burning his belly when him swallow it. Bad enough him must drink the diluted rose wine every first Sunday at Communion.

'Him was sitting down at my bedside. Holding my hand.' Ian's voice fall down to a whisper. 'Something did happen to me. But I can't remember . . .'

Dale didn't even feel when the nurse lady tap him on the shoulder with her pencil. It was upon the second round that him turn to her.

'Your brother?' she ask, pointing in the direction them wheel off with Ian.

'Friend.'

She nod and hand Dale the clipboard with the forms attach.

'Come back tomorrow.'

Dale couldn't place her accent.

'Him in intensive care. Drop off the forms when you leave.'

Then she breeze out as silently as she came in, her shoes white and shine from a fresh coat of whitening.

Before leaving, Dale use the call box out front and phone Ian Kaysen's work. And after that, Bill's place of business. Him didn't bother to call Nevin, but him phone Alexander Pilot and arrange to meet same time as usual, but in front the flowers shop at the Spanish Town Mall instead. Dale buy a bun and cheese sandwich and a small box milk from the handcart vendor nearby and board the bus out to Spanish Town Road where Ian's mother live, for she didn't have a phone.

According to what Nevin told Dale from the time him did meet her, Miss Kaysen is a woman who doesn't believe in the luxuries of life. She would never pick up her good-good money to buy a wristwatch when she can still tell the time by how shadows fall against the sun on any given afternoon or morning. For similar reasons, she would never buy a transistor radio, a television set, or even a telephone. If a storm to come, or even a hurricane, she can tell by the force of the north wind as it whip through her hair that reach way down behind her knees, the dampness of the rain on her tongue, and the depth to the roaring of the thunder as it rattle her zinc roof and shake the chicken coop under the breadfruit tree. She claim that any bit of news she supposed to hear would cause a ringing in her ears from now till next week unless she buck-up on the correct source of contention. Her dreams each night, whether calm or storm, will always reveal whatever bad news telephone going to bring.

Any appliance inside her house is either present she get from people who don't know her very well, who want to bond with her, or nonsense Mr Kaysen spend his decent money and buy. His love for gadgets, she claim, did come before even she. One good thing about the death, she did stand up and tell Nevin, in front of Ian, is that she don't have to worry about the whole heap of electrical things clutter-cluttering her house and building up dust. She did

35

pack up every last one, down to the satellite dish and give it to Mr Kaysen's side of family. Ungrateful wretches didn't even turn the black of them eyes to say thanks, she observe. Only to complain that she is the one who rise-up his blood pressure and cause him to drop down dead from heart attack.

Since she was a woman keep her white gate chain up to keep out those not welcome inside, Dale did have to knock on the bright red mail-box. When that didn't bring her attention, pound on it hard with his entire set of house keys. Seven in all. And then him glance around briefly at the row of concrete houses all with the same mud brown roofs, the same verandah with hanging spider plants, the same white gate and red mail-box, the same small patch of grass to one side, the same neatly trimmed hedges. One house repeated twenty-seven times. Separated by the road. Then repeated twenty-seven more times.

Him didn't know how long she was standing up inside her doorway, hands fold-up crossway her bosom, before she clean her throat.

'No need to mash down the gate, you know. The eyes bad, but I not deaf atall.'

Dale swallow saliva. The woman in front him was the spit image of Ian: tall and stately in a bright yellow house frock; skin as dark as half-roast pimento beans. She still owned all her teeth and her smile when she flash it, pearly and white, didn't smooth-out the hardness in her eyes. And suddenly it occur to Dale that for the five years him been at the church, he'd never yet seen her face, only her back, sturdy like a boulder inside her black frocks, retreating from the churchyard, head to the sky.

'I don't have all day to stand up and form the fool. Get on with the complaint.'

'Ian drop down this morning, mam. Them admit him up at Spaul . . .'

'I can't hear you atall, atall. I don't have on me glasses and I can't see how your mouth lips moving. Start again.'

Dale wonder if she couldn't walk and come to the gate. The sun was raging crossway the sky. Sweat trickle down behind his two ears.

'Ian drop down this morning, and them admit . . .'

36

'By the way. Who are you, sir?' In the middle of the heat, him could hear the chill to her voice.

Dale sigh, temper mounting. 'Dale Singleton, mam.'

'You from around here?'

'No, mam. Country. Saint Elizabeth.'

People were starting to open up windows and peer outside to see who it was causing the commotion this early in the day. 'But me and Ian are good friends. Use to go to the same school.'

'Well, Mister Singleton,' she start to walk out towards the gate, swaying side to side wide hips inside the sleeveless cotton frock. 'Plenty people don't know it, but take it as I tell you. I only have two children left. Courtney and Andrea.'

'Mam?' She did have her face close-up to Dale's. The milk curdle-up into his throat. Him shut his eyes tight and swallow it down.

'Courtney marry now three years and give me a nice grand-daughter seven months ago. Andrea still finishing her studies.' She pause.

Dale smell dry pine and kerosene oil on her breath.

'When your child choose a course God didn't cut out for him, you dish him dirt.' Her voice take on a dull ring. 'You wash your hands clean. You banish him from your life.'

'But his lungs collapse. Him in intensive care,' Dale tell her, adamant, not certain what propelled him out here in the first place, what him was hoping to accomplish.

But she'd already turn her back and was walking towards the house slowly. 'Banishment, me son, banishment.' She whisper it over and over.

Dale remember about the people him see earlier, those sitting on the verandah, puttering in the lawn, and spin around to see if them hear. But every window in sight close-up, every door fasten tight. Him start to run, slow at first, shirt billowing in the slight wind movement. But then the speed pick up as more and more of the conversation filter down new meanings.

And as him run, flashes of his own mother spread crossway his vision. Him squint, trying hard to block them, but them hover around, threatening. Him see her face, broad and round; her narrow nose and fine teeth that scatter around her mouth.

Everybody say them resemble. Same style of walking that has a purpose in each step, same little bit of hair on the body. The few strands Dale had at birth did feather out by now, and even the mother used to wear the same curly wig for sixty straight years.

Him remember the funeral: the mahogany casket pad with blue velvet inside, she'd pick out herself long before the doctor even diagnose her; body stretch out at ease, smelling high of marigold and decay mix together; wig, shampoo and fluff, press down firmly crossway her forehead. A film of white powder mask her face.

It was pouring rain the Sunday and cold, but that didn't stop the turnout. The procession did stretch over two miles behind six pall-bearers who rest the coffin on shoulders padded with white tablecloths. As cars couldn't climb over the rocky dirt road, people either walk single-file or ride bicycles and donkeys. Everybody she know, present. June Mills who still owe her twenty pounds ten, Carlton Marx who'd borrow her swell-up comb red rooster and never returned it, Teacher Rob who wanted to marry her after them father left, and all the people she use to make wedding frocks for. His sister was there, the one who live abroad, the brother him can't stand these days, and the distant uncle who everybody say 'that way.' The father was there too, tall and serene in a brand new black felt hat from England, surrounded by his new family.

Even up to now, Dale still can't tell whether it was from the heat, her sickness, the news, or everything put together that caused her to react that way when him try to come out to her. She was seated on the bed facing the bureau, stocky legs knocking against the sides as she hum some song or other, the white scarf on her head scented high of the bay rum that ease the plenty headaches she get now. Dale did have it well rehearsed.

Niguel Chambers, Dale's best friend, couldn't understand why Dale wanted to tell her atall. 'A mother born and raise you,' him tell Dale while the two play marbles under the heavy branches of a big Julie mango tree. 'If you differ from any of the others, she'd be the first to spot it.'

Still Dale wanted to tell her. Evening time around the small dinette set, his brother would always engage her about which light-skinned girl him was sporting this week. Sister wasn't any different. She was a woman who love to talk at length about the cast-eyed taxi driver she been courting on and off for two straight years. And all that Dale, the oldest, could talk about was his project for the science fair, spelling bee practice and at which Pentecostal church him and the choir plan to perform next.

Now and again, when his mother mention Doris, the girl him walk to school with some mornings, his brother always elbow him, the smile on his face, devilish, the jab to Dale's ribs painstaking. But Dale didn't feel comfortable talking about her. Neither about Precious or even Winsome. For it didn't spell sense talking about them, especially when that glow didn't shadow his eyes like when his sister talk about Audley. When him think about the girls in his class, the ones that sit down beside him in geometry or even Spanish, certain warm feelings didn't creep down into his middle section and stretch out his trousers like what seem to always happen to other boys.

Not that there was a particular fellow causing him to walk round starry-eyed, or to lose appetite, sigh loud and sleep plenty like people in love. But sometimes in the dead of the night when the moon slip under; when toads' eyelids close over; and his brother snore hearty on the next twin bed; boys alone fill his mind, sending out each breath in such quick gulps, him have to muffle the sounds underneath the pillow, rubbing himself desperately till peace come again. Not so much the tough raucous boys him play cricket against on Thursday afternoons, or the jocks heavy with veins him shower with after soccer practice, but the tall, slender ones in the choir wearing black suits and sparkling white shoes him sway against on Sundays.

As a result, Dale strike up friendship with both the librarian and school psychiatrist. Them became so close, the librarian learned to expect him Tuesdays and Thursdays at exactly seven minutes past ten and would offer Dale the other half of his egg-and-cheese sandwich which Dale would always take, tell him thanks, but would never eat. Left-over questions that psychology texts and medicine journals couldn't respond to adequately enough, Dr Lewis would explain at length and in great detail, his light grey eyes shifting tenderly around the box-shaped little office, never once making contact with Dale's.

Dale felt well prepared for the mother. Any questions she have, concerns or simple misunderstandings, him was more than ready to clear up right away with a long list of references from which him could cite.

'You know what them say about Uncle Ralph, Mama?' Him approach her one afternoon, hands press against thighs, head held-up high, way over-confident.

She continue to hum, eyes close, head swaying slow, beads of sweat on her forehead, face shine. And inside, the room shimmered with the smells of Limecol and Bayrum and Aloes, old and unwashed clothes and perspiration.

'You know, that him funny that way.' Him did pause, waiting for her eyes to flutter open, the rhythm stop in her humming, the foot cease from slapping against the side of the four-poster bed that stood four feet from the floor on sturdy iron legs with claws. But nothing atall. Him continue to wait for her attention, sweat sliding down the crease in his back, before nestling itself between the part in his behind. 'I'm that way too.' Him did talk down into his neck, clammy with dirt, into the striped shirt collar, muffling the sound.

But she still collapse. Faint way. Fold over, limp. The head nestling in her lap. Him start to shake the shoulders, limp inside the purple house dress, rub her back with circular gestures, kiss her damp tie-head, bitter with rubbings, tell her him didn't mean it, is only a phase him going through, it bound to stop. But it didn't bring her to.

Not long after, the sister revive her with a bottle of horse-power salts wavering underneath her nose. Recognition fall back into her eyes. Her face look fresh and vibrant again. The muscles in her neck jerk around, erratic. But not a word about it mention.

Outside the flowers shop, sandwich between two Checker taxis, Alexander's blue Buick wait patiently. It was always spotless inside, never a speck of dirt, or lint, a crumpled piece of paper. Even with two young children. Always shiny on the outside. And this afternoon with the sky a hazy silver, the light white and diffused, the Buick shimmered more than ever in the heat. The oppressive and unbearable mid-afternoon heat.

'She mad!' Dale say to him first thing, slamming the car door shut, oblivious to Alexander's wince, and winding down the window, hurriedly, furiously, as if wanting to tear off the handle. 'My mother wouldn't agree with everything we do, but she would never forsake us in the eyes of trouble. In the face of sickness.' Him pause, eyes bleary, filmy with the images of Miss Kaysen, the conversation, his mother.

'Ian won't admit it. But the woman crazy! She send back everything him give her. She disown him cause him can't give her children. Cause him won't marry. Cause him love man. Man!' Dale pound his leg with his fist, lips trembling, eye water in his voice, the crab solemn.

Then him turn to Alexander who'd remain silent throughout the entire pandemonium. 'You'd disown Junior if him turn out batty man? Bar his sweetheart from coming to your house? Stop supporting him?' Dale wait, anger subsiding, annoyance building instead. Him hate the hesitancy, the slowness of speech, the biding of time, the silence. Sometimes him was certain Alexander do it on purpose, to rile him, make him hot-hot.

'Well, no. Not really.'

'What you mean not really?' Dale's forehead fold over into a furrow. 'What kind of answer that?' Him watch the hands, hairy and crab-like, on the steering wheel. The nails coarse, claw-like. They weren't delicate, soft with rounded tips and half moons like Nevin's. Dale's eyes trail down to the stomach brushing against the steering. It ripple every time Alexander laugh.

'I'd rather him get married. Have a family.'

'And stay closet like you.'

The car slow down at the lights. A whole host of schoolchildren and old people cross the street with the guide, a tall, stringy fellow dress-up in white.

Alexander look over at Dale, voice calm, soothing. 'Sounds like Ian's sickness upset you bad.' His right hand slide off the steering and fall into Dale's lap. 'Looks like the mother didn't take to the news too good atall.' It crawl gingerly up and down inside one thigh, linger for a while, before gliding gently up and down inside the other thigh. 'Parents not easy to get on with. You have to be careful how you approach them.' The lights turn green and with

41

the left hand, Alexander manoeuvre the car gracefully through Spanish Town Road traffic to the usual destination.

Inside the dingy little back room that Alexander rent from the woman for fifty dollars each month, Dale fold up his linen trousers neatly over the back of the grimy metal chair and position himself gingerly on the king-size water-bed. Behind him, Alexander lock and bolt the door and pull the shades over the one narrow window that overlook the woman's clothesline laden with her husband's short sleeve Arrow shirts whitened with blue, and his khaki trousers pinned upside down with ink spots dotting the flour bag pockets. Then Alexander tear off his plaid trousers, toss them restlessly on the dirt brown carpet before hopping on to the bed with Dale.

But Dale wasn't in the mood for love. Him wanted to go home to the safe walls of Nevin's apartment and curl up under the thin sheets of his cot with the pillows pull over his head. Him wanted to howl out loud, for all of a sudden him was really missing his mother, and it wasn't fair what Miss Kaysen was doing to Ian and this was not what him wanted to be doing right now. But him didn't know how to tell Alexander. Once him did try. It was early into the relationship, the third time Alexander had brought him to the room. Him did like it the first time, something about it felt risky, dangerous, for once him feel as if him did have the upper hand on Nevin. But by the second time, all the romance fell away dead. And all of a sudden Alexander seemed vile to him and reminded Dale very much of his father whose jet black eyes would always caress the tail of every young girl him see without a care if anyone noticed.

That night Dale did lie inside the tub, trying to absolve himself with handfuls of baking soda and Epsom salts poured into the hot and perfumed water. Him did promise himself never to go back, to call Alexander and say it was over. But Dale didn't call, and the third time him and Alexander meet, him did follow Alexander's wide and flattened behind slowly up the battered stairs of the old house as usual, not quite trusting to hold on to the shaky wooden banisters, just in case it gave way.

Inside the room with the door bolt, him couldn't remove his clothes. Alexander was lively and humorous as usual, telling Dale some joke or other about the woman with whom him share his office at school. But Dale couldn't laugh, him wanted to leave, him wanted the relationship to go back to the way it had been. Him wanted the walks again through Hope botanical gardens, with Alexander in the lead, pointing out various trees, naming flowers, and the trips to the museums downtown.

'Alexander, I don't want to do this any more.' It flew out in a much louder and hardened voice than Dale had expected. Silence filled the room and Dale couldn't meet his face, the placid lemon-coloured face with horn-rimmed glasses, his once lively green eyes now gone deadpan. Dale's eyes stopped instead at the curly tufts of grey that spill out at the V of the short sleeve polyester shirt encircling the buttons. 'It's just that I still have a lover. I didn't mean for this to happen all the time. I . . .'

'OK. Then we'll stop.' Alexander's tone was final. Him stoop down to tie his shoes lace. And again Dale was left to grapple with the silence in the room, Alexander's slow breathing, his balding head, and the tinny sounds from a transistor radio playing Mento outside somewhere.

'Alexander . . .'

'It's OK, Dale.' His tone was carefree enough, but Dale could hear the coldness and hurt seeping through.

Dale walk quickly toward him, and reach out his hand to gently touch him on the shoulder, but Alexander who was tucking his shirt carefully into the mouth of his trousers, eyes expressionless, suddenly pulled back, his face stony, and Dale's hand was left outstretched, grabbing at nothing.

'What the hell you want from me, Dale?'

Dale shake his head and turn away, tears coming to his eyes all of a sudden.

For two months straight Dale didn't see him. It was Mrs Pilot who would drop off the boys on Sundays. And against her Dale would compare himself. The dark grey suits, even on Sundays. Her figure, oversized like Alexander's. Of course, there was still Nevin, and Dale try to preoccupy himself with classes, with church and young people's meeting, with Mrs Morgan. But Alexander was gone. And with him the lectures them used to attend, the visits to Arawak museums where Alexander would explain the significances of the slight indentations in certain carved items with such authority and simplicity, almost as if him did know personally the fellow who carved the piece, did discuss the project with him over plenty enamel mugs filled with warm brandy. Also gone, was a certain kind of articulateness Alexander had, that Nevin didn't quite possess; Alexander's knowledge about art; his advice about school; his gentle mannerisms; his curiosity; and his sweet gentleness with his children that reminded Dale so much of what him couldn't get from his father.

Yes, church was Dale's pride and joy, without it, him probably would be like a lost ship on stormy waters, floundering helplessly, no compass to steer him right. But the people were narrow-minded, too fundamental, the course them carve out too rigid. There wasn't one person there with whom him could discuss a book, or a show, a piece of art for them didn't live lives outside the church. Maybe one or two of the late-teenage members, but him didn't want to strike up too close a friendship with any of them, for one thing would lead to another and then them would want to know why him didn't have a girlfriend, who was this man, Nevin, that him live with, and Dale wouldn't quite know what to tell them. Him was tired of lying.

And so when Alexander returned two months later to drop off his sons at Sunday School, Dale just lap his tail between his legs and proceeded to pick up from where them did leave off. But him couldn't kiss any more. Had suddenly lost the desire. And it made Alexander very angry. Inside the room, Dale cough dry, hating himself, not wanting to succumb to the desires battering against his chest, bubbling like hot water in his ears, creating havoc in his breathing. But his body had grown accustomed to Alexander's caresses. Him try to think about his history assignment due. Miss Kaysen. The frowsy little room, rank with the scent of wet newspaper and stale sex; Alexander's snores when them finish: mouth slightly ajar; penis shiny, limp, lean over sideways; clothes in a puddle on the floor at the foot of the bed; the one grungy towel fling one side; Dale's trousers hung neat over the back of the metal chair.

But the thoughts didn't linger long in any one particular direction, for the fingers kneading his crotch strangle all sense of logic and clarity, enveloping him instead with the smell of old spice and sweat. The room take on a sudden brilliance, orchestral arrangements, breathing bursting out in spurts. The gold pendant that nestle the hollow at the base of Alexander's throat, graze Dale's neck, trail alongside earlobes, slide in and out between his lips. Him feel Alexander's tongue wet, prodding, as it dart into the hollow of nostrils, circle up over eyelids, linger by temples, entangling itself among the folds of Dale's softness.

That night, try as him might, Dale couldn't sleep a wink. Every time his eyelids flutter shut, all him could see behind him was Ian alone in the hospital room, makeshift curtains separating him from the half-dead person on the next twin bed. Probably wake up in the middle of the night, confused at first, wondering why the bed so hard, why him feeling so stiff, slipping back into unconscious when him come to remember.

The little cot sag heavy under Dale's weight. It creak with every turn, every gesture. If Nevin was home, Dale would crawl into his bed and underneath the cover, raise up Nevin's elbow and slip inside the curve. Nevin would hug him close, pressing his stomach on to Dale's back as them spoon, body scents familiar. Dale wonder where and with whom him was tonight.

Him couldn't call up Alexander. Not at two in the morning, and wake up the wife and children. Although him wouldn't mind causing a little trouble, stir-up suspicion inside the wife. It bother him, the way Alexander would rather if Dale just chat and laugh and act as if nothing atall would discombobulate him. Him have it hard forgetting the night him did call Alexander right after another big quarrel with Nevin. That night he'd just wanted somebody to hold him. Squeeze him tight. Advise as to what must be done. Just three days before him and Alexander spent two whole days together. Mrs Pilot was gone with the two boys to country. Back up at the little wooden house them did rent for the few days with the cows and goats out back, whatever Alexander chop-up and peel, Dale put in the pot and stir around. Them did seem so close.

45

But when Dale call him three o'clock the morning, all the closeness drop way sudden.

'Don't ever call me house those hours of the morning and wake up Doris and the children again,' Alexander grind out inside the restaurant the next day, for that night him simply tell Dale him was busy, can't come to the phone right now, and hang up sudden. 'What you have with Nevin, keep it to yourself. What I have with Doris stay between me and she.'

Dale did look at him, eyes surprise. No words atall falling from his lips. For after all what him could possibly say.

But after noticing a kind of sadness shadowing Dale's eyes, Alexander did put down his fork and touch Dale's hand. 'I don't want Doris to find out and spoil things.' His voice was softer, more kind. 'When we spend time together, I want it to be fun. Me and you just enjoying one another's company. Our haven of happiness.'

Dale did only smile and nod slowly, hating Alexander with a passion, this hot and cold business.

Inside the study, Dale draw the curtains shut, clear the newspaper clippings from off the desk, open-up a Geography book and try to read. But him didn't budge further than the first paragraph. Him listen as each car drive by, waiting for it to slow down and pull into the gate. Out the window, banana trees sway slow with each wind movement, resembling couples holding hands in the dark.

A light burn still inside Mrs Morgan's office window. Dale figure she was probably sitting up on the stool around the table reading. It always puzzle him the books and magazines she have pack away on the metal shelves: Thompson's guide to designing home-made hand grenades; how to make money and keep it; laying pipes for irrigation; running underground electrical wiring for entire communities . . .

Dale wasn't sure if him wanted to spend time with her tonight. She was so sometimish. One day, chat and laugh from now till next week as if you and she coming from afar. Another time, you go over to borrow a handful of salt. And instead of inviting you inside, offering a cup of orange leaf tea like last week, she meet you in the doorway instead, give you the entire box full she have, and tell you not to come back, she wasn't running Chin's Supermarket. Nonetheless, Dale haul on trousers, put on shoes, scale the fence and go over. Him didn't want to stay in tonight. Not by himself. Lonesome. Without somebody to talk to.

'Dale, is you that? Knocking down me door this ungodly hour of the morning?' Mrs Morgan haul open the door with her foot and fan him to the couch lean up on four milk crates against the wall. 'I hear you over there walking around. Switching off one light bulb, turning on another. You not a quiet man, atall. Things on your mind.'

Him try to decipher her tone of voice. If she was glad to see him or just plain annoyed, but she didn't raise her eyes to look at him once. Her face glisten shine from the heat and glare of the bulb hanging not far from her head. The table in front her was piled high with paper.

'I don't mean to bother you . . .'

'Cho!' She hand him a pile of papers hold together with a piece of elastic. 'Here, look through these and pick out all the ones for 1977. You want a little ginger tea?'

Dale shake his head. She slurp a mouthful from her mug.

'Can't allow them to audit me again like last time. I don't have it to fling away and give government.' She cough dry, rustling with her foot another heap of papers yellowing with age piled up on the floor.

Dale make himself comfortable on the couch, not sure if him should start first or to leave it up to Mrs Morgan.

'I notice a new car out the gate now and again,' she start off. 'It doesn't seem to linger long. Just enough to drop off till next time.'

Dale shift round, uncertain how him should answer. Him glance at her posture – rigid inside the red nightie, two thin straps holding up her breasts in order. A stick of lead pencil stand up in her hair. Him decide against answering. The two of them big people. If she want to know something, she should ask. Stop this go around and come around business.

'Sort of heavy around the middle,' she continue, since Dale

47

wasn't rising to the bait. 'Balding out up top. Shortish. Gold ring on his married finger.'

For a woman who don't look at people much, she notice plenty. 'Oh, Alexander!' Him manage it with a tone of purposeful indifference. 'Friend from church.'

'Hmmmh.' She study the receipt in her hand.

'Wife teach up at my school.'

That seem to satisfy her, she move on, voice little bit more kind. 'Then how school?'

But she didn't wait for an answer. 'Lord. I wish Rose would go back. For she have a good head. Quick as lightning. Teacher Polish say she'd go on to big things. But all Rose want to study is that blasted Rastaman, Barry.' She pause, adjusting the eyeglasses perch crooked on her nose, one bow bandage up with duck tape.

'And all that good-for-nothing do each day is smoke-up the ganja and chat nonsense in her ears hole. Set him setting to marry her, you know. So him can get the house and the little bit of money I have save-up at the bank.' Mrs Morgan turn around to peer at Dale as if him know already about the conspiracy against her. She and Nevin have the same dirt brown eyes, except one of hers have a tendency to just slide past over your head, beside you, not quite in focus. She turn back to her receipts. 'But I have news for that no count wretch. Him don't even come from good family. Woman inside the market tell me him come from a long line of old thieves. Up Grove Place area.'

Dale swallow sudden. Him did have family up that way.

'But eh. I just talking, talking.' She pause, head cock to one side. 'Where Nevin?'

Dale shrug.

'Still don't figure out how to keep him home, yet.' She chuckle under her breath, sounds rumbling out from deep down inside her belly, knocking up against the one window in the room that look out on to the dark cloudless night, a star here and there, winking then disappearing. 'It's not easy, son. When me and Mr Morgan marry, I was about four months pregnant with Rose.

'But must be Mr Morgan did a sweetheart live up in TopHill. For every Friday after him get pay, him used to go up to TopHill. Talking about him have family up there. Yet, still them never one

48

day send howdy-do or ask after the baby.' She stop, kick off her fluffy red bed slippers, cock up one foot on the stool and start to pick her purple toe-nails, wincing whenever she tear near flesh.

'My father come over one Sunday morning bright and early, pound up two ackee seeds inside the mortar, mix it up with salt and sugar and a dusting of a thing him keep in a pouch latch-on to his waist. Tell me to sprinkle it on his dinner every fortnight for three months. Well, see him there. Shrivel up inside the wheel chair.' The rumble leap out from inside her belly again, vibrating against the window, jarring on Dale's nerves.

Dale shift around nervous on the couch, receipts in a neat pile on his lap. The problem with talking to Mrs Morgan is him could never tell sometimes if she offering advice, telling damn lie, if him should take her serious any atall. His eyes, flooded, wandered the unswept concrete floor, pausing at gaps patch-up with pieces of newspaper, a rag, or larger ones filled in with cement but hadn't been sanded to match smoothly with the remaining surface of floor.

'Things on your mind, plenty.' She turn to him, toe-nails finish pick.

Dale nod, uncertain as to whether or not him should start to say anything or if him should just wait till she launch on again.

'You remember Ian, Mrs Morgan?'

She cock her head one side, thinking. The wandering eye steadfast on Dale's nose.

'Tall, thin . . .'

'That Indian fellow. Resemble woman.' Rumble.

'Him drop down today.'

'Drop down. Fancy!' Her voice ring pity, lilting at the end, face concern. 'Heart?'

'No, mam. Lungs. Them collapse.'

'Fancy that.' Lilt. She pick up her pipe from underneath more papers and start to knock it against her hand middle striped with thin dark lines, eyes travelling up to the corner of the wall, along the cracks, across the ceiling, finally settling on the grey water marks. 'Young boy as that.'

'Just drop down sudden. Not even a little complaint beforehand.'

Mrs Morgan shake her head slow, the yellow lead pencil wavering. She push back the stool with a loud scrape on the concrete, and pace around the room, movements light, easy, contrary to her height and size, pamphlets stash every which way, peeping out of every corner, hanging over the lip of every drawer. 'It don't sound good atall.' Her voice sound like it was coming from outside. 'That means that water probably get down in there. Consumption, like.' She spin around, one sparkling eye settling on Dale's face, the other solemn one on his blue shirt pocket. 'Cough and spit plenty?'

'Cough mostly. Little bit of blood mix in when him spit.' Dale's voice get misty. 'You think it's serious, Mrs Morgan?'

She didn't answer right away. She walk over and stand up in front of him, arms akimbo, breasts flat against her chest, eyes to one corner of the room, her pores vigorous with the scent of ginger and turpentine. 'Him owe money?' Her voice was low, a whisper.

'Mam?'

'You know, have debt? Can't pay it back right away.'

'I don't know.' Dale couldn't quite make sense of what she saying.

'What about enemy? People have him up in them crop?'

Dale shake his head.

'Family love him? Him and them get on?'

'Well . . .' The image of Miss Kaysen loom life-like in front of him. 'The mother doesn't like him much.'

There was a long length of silence. She breathe deep. Walk back to her desk, steps pensive, and put down the pipe quietly. 'Fancy!' Her voice trail off into the ceiling. 'Cause him womanish.'

Dale wasn't quite sure how she arrive at that conclusion, but him didn't say a word.

'Back in my young gal days, I used to know a woman.' She sounded far away again. 'Lovely lady. College teacher. Well respected and successful in her vocation. Church going. Choir singing. All in all decent. She never marry. Did share a flat with another lady. Decent just like herself.' She stop, search inside the front drawer for a box of matches, hands coming up empty. 'Father wasn't happy atall. No matter how she try to please him. Rebuild his house. Buy him a long car. Pay off his debts. Daddy still wasn't content.' She fumble around inside the drawers again, fingers, crooked with arthritis, searching more diligent. 'She move away with her friend to another town. But not far enough it seems. For that man used to still bother her about her ways. Write her letters, send telegram to her school. Next thing you know, she meagre down to nothing. Jaw bone stick out, eyes sink in, teeth drop out one by one. Last time me hear that gal end up inside alms house, poor as church mouse.'

Silence fill the little room. Dale think about Ian's face on the stretcher. Ashen. Jaw kind of slack; lips part slightly as if about to say something. Blood trickle slow from a small gash where his forehead hit the floor. Tears burn behind Dale's nose, the crab tremble.

'But Dale, God not sleeping. Take it as I tell you. Him don't always answer right away when you call. But him listening.' She hop off her stool again. 'Cho, man, Dale. Wipe up the eye water. Don't bother with it atall.' But Dale didn't have any stop to stop. Him bury his head inside his lap, receipts brush to one side, and start up the cow bawling.

'Done, now. Done.' Mrs Morgan bend down in front of him, voice tender. 'All right, done.' She cradle his head inside her lap and use the tail of her dusty red nightie to wipe his face. 'All right now. No mind. You frighten.' She massage his neck with coarse hands clammy with sweat. 'Done now.' She rub his head.

'You have to live blessed, Dale.' She talk down into his collar, her false teeth clicking in his ears. 'You can't just do unto others and expect you won't meet your Waterloo. That woman's father is as mad as shark today. Run around naked and tear up newspaper into bitty scraps.' She pause. 'You just give punch time to ripe and see what happen to that boy's mother. Merlene Kaysen. For she never used to be that way, Dale. No, she was never the kind of person you laugh with easy, never the kind of person you would want around your table at Sunday dinner, but something happen. Yes something happen.' She shake her head. 'Ever since the husband pass, Dale, something happen.' She take off her glasses and use her hand-back to wipe her bulbous brown eyes.

End of April 1978

I

Them release Ian from out the hospital not long after, saying him need plenty rest, lots of fresh air, no more cigarette smoking and haul and pulling of the body. Hardly a day pass when Dale didn't go to see him up at Spauldings General. Standing with the nurses and doctors, him watch as them wring hands and shake heads, narrow eyes fold over perplexed at the nature of the illness. The nurse lady Dale pull one side didn't have much to say. No, she didn't see any particular puncture hole, so it can't be asthma or any kind of lung abscess. But X-ray results will come out next week. She can't understand herself what cause the pain in the chest and shoulder area. What exactly him spitting up in such abundance. Maybe pneumonia, but them still drawing blood and testing. Bill did bring Ian home the morning along with all the get-well bouquets and store-wrap chocolate.

It was pouring rain the evening Nevin and Dale drive over to see him. All along Red Hills Road, cars, buses, six-wheel trailer trucks back-up behind one another, tyres slicing through thick, heavy mud. Road block, the news trickle down from the plain clothes police man directing traffic. One hand resting gently on Dale's lap, the other on steering wheel, Nevin whistle softly his own tunes, fingers tapping lightly. Inside the car, fan stir hot air. Radio, Country and Western from the rear as them move on bumper to bumper. The wiper slide lazily across windshield cloudy with fog and muffler smoke.

Seat push back, legs stretch forward, Dale stare on, looking at nothing in particular, relishing the memory of the last few days.

Him did only go for the ride, for the thought of spending long length of time with Mrs Morgan's side of family didn't bring him joy and comfort.

Him did expect to just drop off the barrel-full of canned goods, soap and old clothes Mrs Morgan usually post off every six months and turn right around. But when them reach Nevin wanted to show Dale the pond where him used to swim naked as a boy and dig-up worms and slugs to use as bait to catch fish. Him show Dale the field, cover over with bramble, where him use to play soccer; the school him go for seventeen months before them move. It shut down now and all the windows either break or thief-out. Guinea grass grow wild around the door mouth. The rancid smell of something dead hang heavy in the air.

'I have something to ask you.' Nevin break the silence. 'I want you think about it careful. Is a subject that cause plenty contention between me and you in the past.'

Dale only half heard him. Head leaning to one side, eyes barely in focus with the truck driver on his right, him think about the tenderness that had grown between him and Nevin the past few days. The last time they'd made love or even held each other close was three months ago, on Nevin's 35th birthday, but last night as them pick ticks off one another in Nevin's cousin's four-poster bed, fingers probing into places not so familiar any more, old feelings had returned and like poignant memories, suffused them.

'You interested in the store?'

Dale's body stiffen. Coldness seep over his chest. 'How you mean, interested?'

'To run it. You know, help out.'

'No.' Dale couldn't understand why Nevin wanted to spoil things now. The last few days seemed so hopeful. Nevin was open, relaxed. It made Dale think that maybe there was hope for them, that since the foundation was strong enough, maybe them could overlook the problems.

'Hear me out first, Dale.'

'No.'

Up ahead, cars started to move. Nevin raised his hand off Dale's lap, put the car into first, then second. First again as them meet with crowds of people demonstrating. It didn't faze them any.

This was common accord during election time. Them wind up the windows and lock the doors. 'Thinking about branching out.' The burdensome moustache twitched. 'Maybe we could market some of the things you sew and crochet. We could co-own it. Me and you run it together.'

'What about Johnney?' It slip out even before Dale could consider.

The car lurch. Charlie Pride belt out another tune. A man punch the car with his fist and scream out something at them, eyes red. The windows grow cloudy.

'I can fire him. If you want. But it doesn't make sense. Him know the business. I would have to hire somebody else. Train them all over again. Start from scratch.'

Maybe it was the way him said it, voice calm with the irritation and scorn straining through. The way the vein just pop out by his temple, only when him cross. The way the lines by his lips tighten. But it rile Dale to no ends. Flare out his nostrils and tighten the edges of his mouth. It cause his eyes to squeeze down to slits. 'Especially since you have him well trained already.'

'Dale, him straight.'

'That didn't stop you. You still pick him up, clean him up and let him run your shop.'

Nevin's top lip quiver under the moustache. His forehead glisten shine from where hair was beginning to recede. 'You were the first one I thought about when I open that shop. But you just started school. You were going full time. Every evening you used to come home with more and more work.'

'Fucking lie. The only reason that boy's in the store is cause you want him. So don't give me this shit about me. As if you concern. As a matter of fact, let me out. I will walk. Can't bear to sit down and listen to a fucking liar.' Dale lift the catch and start to open the door. The crowd had moved forward, past the car. Debris flow free along the roadway. Nevin reach over and grab him. The car swerve into the other lane. Tyres screech from behind. Horns hoot. Nevin steady the steering wheel.

The announcer's voice ring crystal over the speakers. She mention the road block, the fifteen demonstrators who had to be forcibly removed from outside the Governor General's house, the new labour proposal Mr Manley put before the Cabinet, how the rain will continue on all through till tomorrow morning, which racehorse win at Kaymannis Park . . .

Dale stare out the window, eyes unseeing. The party come back to him. The store-warming surprise get-together him give Nevin not long after Nevin branch off from Mrs Morgan and open his own store down Silver Lane Plaza. Dale post off twenty invitations. Over fifty people turn up. To this day, him still don't know who invite Johnney. Nevin did run in surprise, everybody dress up in white dinner jacket and black bow tie, him alone in a pair of khaki trousers, white mesh-marine and sneakers. Face beaming, Nevin run over to Dale and hug him. Start to cry, silent eye water that drip down into Dale's collar, leaving salt brine on his neck.

Dale did only squeeze his hand, face quiet. But inside him see himself and Nevin in the store, side by side around the counter, making change give customers, telling them which colour fabric best suit them skin, exactly how many yards of khaki could make school uniforms for size six boys, which material them must careful only wash in warm, sudsy water. Him see them around the kitchen table, mug-full of mint tea in hand, going over reports and plans; in a three-bedroom up in Stoney Hill, far away as possible from underneath Mrs Morgan's deep scrutiny.

The function ran late into the evening. Dale back way into the kitchen, tired and thirsty, for a glass of plain ice water. Him push open the window for a little fresh air, stretching himself half-way outside into the night, barely any stars atall in sight. It seem far away, the laughing, the clinking of ice against glass, low voices droning.

The glowing of the cigarette in the darkness draw his attention. The sudden brightness before it dulled again. Curling of the smoke in the still night air. His chest constrict and the air burst out in gulps as him come to realise it was Nevin outside lean up against the column. And it wasn't who him stand-up out there with or what them choose to talk about in the darkness far away from everybody else that concern Dale. Is was the way him stand-up. For it wasn't the kind of pose that suggest a friendly cup of coffee now and again, or even come over for dinner and taste Dale's good cooking, him did lean up against the column, shoulders fling back, arms clasp crossway his chest, pelvic thrust forward.

Dale pull in himself, shut down the window, squeeze back the burning behind his nose and start to mingle with the crowd again. Him didn't have another word to utter to Nevin for the remainder of the night. All of a sudden it became clear that Nevin's kisses didn't belong to just him anymore. His lips press against other fellows' mouths, alongside navels, between thighs with just as much fervency; just as much ferocity. Now and again, Dale would find himself searching through each one of Nevin's trousers pocket for crumple-up pieces of napkin that have a telephone number or address scrawl on to it. Saturday mornings as him sort clothes for laundry, his nose linger inside each shirt collar waiting for a cologne not so familiar; a different body sweat. Him didn't understand where him went wrong, if his face was starting to age; if him wasn't offering Nevin enough support in his work; if them plans for life were just too different; if him just couldn't satisfy Nevin any more. The appeals to the mother each night, for guidance and strength did pick-up in frequency.

'You can't take it to heart,' Mrs Morgan assure him, after Dale – fed up and confuse – did go to her for help. Him wasn't certain how to bring it up, the evening the two of them sit down under the mango tree and sip orange leaf tea. But him didn't feel confident bringing it up with some of the hypocrites him and Nevin share as friends. Him did ask her politely how she'd manage if Mr Morgan openly keep woman with her.

'Can't do more than wait it out, me love. Any sensible woman will tell you that. Most men just like damn dogs. For no matter how much you treat a dog good: give it place to lie down sleep when night come; give it plenty food; the minute it see another dog, its skin catch afire. Ears perk. Mouth spring water. Next thing you know it run gone. Sniff-sniff under somebody else frock-tail. Hop on to somebody else back. But it will come back. Nine times out of ten. For it's mindful of the hand that feed it.'

Weeks later when Nevin mentioned that him hire the boy to run the store, tone flip and matter-of-fact as him sit at the breakfast table eating eggs sunny side-up, Dale behind him squeezing oranges, Dale's eyes suddenly got dark and still.

'What?' Dale put down the orange in his hand and turn to face Nevin's neck back.

Nevin repeat it, voice just as sparkling as the weather man predict for the day.

'After me pick out the location, think up the name and decide on the colour scheme, you going to put this boy in there? That little shit tail boy, you don't even know?' Dale stop sudden. His right hand reach inside the drawer and into the tray. His hand circle the dry wooden handle of the ice pick, caressing it.

Three years with Nevin just didn't mean much, anymore. Him did give up the scholarship to study abroad, with his friend Niguel, the insurance work over Balaclava that promise big money. All because Nevin didn't want him to leave. Now this was the thanks. The gratitude. Somebody new was taking over. Nevin was dashing him aside. Like his mother had left him. And his father before her. That morning, Dale felt as if the whole world was whirling crazy around him. For if Nevin wasn't there anymore, who was going to believe in him? Who was there for him to cling to? Who would make him feel safe? Dale did see his father all over again, standing tall and stout in the police uniform, grinning down at the postmistress beside him, his mother looking on in the background.

Nevin continue to cut up bread into tiny, white squares, knife and fork squeaking on the china. But must be him did sense it, the sudden stillness in the room, the hammering inside Dale's chest, Mrs Morgan outside humming, for him spin around just in time. Thrust up against the cabinet, then the stove, then knock over kettle, turn over chairs and shatter the vase lean up in the corner with the hundreds of one-cents.

Dale hit the floor first, screaming hysterical, Nevin beside him calm, talking reason. One second Dale fling Nevin flat on his back, shaking the floor, rattling the few pieces of china on the wall, breaking one or two, next minute Nevin lay down on top, hugging him, telling him is all right, trying his best to finagle the ice pick from out Dale's hand.

The psychiatrist lady Dale went to right after the incident didn't have much more to say barring Dale must get out of the relationship quick-and-brisk. She say it in her usual soft-spoken, nonchalent, mannish voice. She say it from her high back chair across the room facing Dale. She say it while her fingers twist and turn inside her lap like cripples.

'How?' Dale ask, annoyed that she couldn't come up with a more feasible solution, an easier way. 'Just pack up my things and leave? After just one fight?'

'Was that the first one?' Dr Barnaby peer at Dale through night dark eyes, slanted at the wings.

Dale look down at his fingers. 'No. But nothing as big as this. Nothing where I was ever so angry at him. Nothing where I ever wanted to . . . kill him.' Dale stop and cradle his head in his hands. Nevin's face loom large before him, eyes wide, frightened, the centipede bristling with the tension in the room. Him didn't know where the power had come from all of a sudden, causing him to grab the ice pick. Him wasn't a violent person. While his younger brother would always get involved in fights at school, Dale hadn't so much as raised his voice. Him was always kind to dumb things, always willing to help, volunteer his assistance. Several boys did gather around to beat him up once, on the playfield, because according to them, him was too 'sissyish'.

But Dale didn't do anything more than just sit down and wait, for this was part of the burden him was supposed to carry. Them did beat him up, knock out one of his corner teeth, sprain several of his fingers, but Dale didn't utter out a sound louder than his whimpers for help. His father and mother used to quarrel. Day and night, it seems. But never when Dale and the other two were in sight. Sometimes late at night Dale would hear them, though, hushed tones rising and falling like trapped steam, from out the master bedroom, his mother's tone twisted with anger, his father's, stolid, noncommital. But not once had the father ever lifted his hand to strike her. So where this sudden urge came from to kill, to commit ill, was beyond him.

'Tell me about Johnney,' Dr Barnaby break into his thinking, adjusting the small box pleats of her floral skirt with ringed and stubby fingers. 'How old is he? What's he like? Why do you think Nevin takes a shine to him?'

Dale shrug, shoulders slump down inside the chair, hands clasp

58

between his knees. Him could see Nevin and the boy now, on the little blue couch in the back of the store, 'soon come back' sign hang askew from the door. Bare-face, the boy wouldn't know quite exactly what to do; how to start. But Nevin would teach him – the way him teach Dale – for him gentle and patient that way.

Nevin didn't have the store yet when him and Dale first met. Used to work alongside the mother in the market selling calico cloth and crinolene. Dale was eighteen going on. Just graduate from khaki shorts to trousers. Thighs used to lump out through them like thirty-five cents loaves of hard-dough bread. Them days, Dale used to practise with the cricket team every evening after school. People would park cars close by, walk over near the bleachers, perch-up on the wooden stands, and watch, hands tight in pockets. Them used to pick up and throw back the balls that bat way past the boundaries.

The man used to watch from the car: sometimes through the window wind-down halfway; other times from the hood hoist-up. One day when the ball settle not far from the fender, him did open the door, leap outside, pick it up and fling it back. But not before Dale catch the gleam that lighten his eyes, youthen his face and cause the scar by his mouth corner to quiver.

When Dale point him out to Niguel, ask what him think, Niguel nod his agreement.

'How you know?' It use to irritate Dale sometimes, Niguel's constant wealth of knowledge, opinions, advice.

'Watch the movements,' Niguel tell him, cocky-like. 'The message in the walk. Notice who him glance at first when him look at people, follow the eyes. And most important,' Niguel instruct him, 'notice the batty man trousers him wearing. Not a single, solitary pocket.'

For two straight weeks Dale plan and strategise ways to meet him, things to say to the man, who was starting to come two evenings a week. Before it was only one. Always dress-up in white, face bearded, hair neat – prematurely greying at the temples, a gold bracelet dangling from thick wrist. One evening after practice, everybody else marching back towards the school, Dale did walk up to him. Flattery always work, Niguel champion him on.

'You must be a cricket pro?' Dale did ask, swinging the bat

nervous-like, flexing the muscles in his hand, showing off taut, stone-like skin. Him well know from the way the man fling back the ball, the way his posture lumber crooked, the way his elbow curve when it suppose to straighten, that him probably couldn't even run fast. 'Most every evening you come and watch.' Up close, Dale did want to run his finger alongside the scar.

'Can't play to knock a dog.' The voice was deep, husky. Just the way Dale imagine. Him smell of musk oil. And what a pair of sexy bedroom eyes!

'And bowl a ball like that?' Dale perch himself up on the seat below, face turn toward him, looking upward. 'You bowl almost as good as the players at Lord's.'

The man grin. Showing two small dimples. Him didn't seem as old, must be the beard, or the moustache that weigh down his chin. The skin around the eyes and forehead seem unwrinkled, delicate. Him wasn't exactly good-looking.

'You like to pull people's legs?' The tone was silky, seductive-like.

Dale turned away. Hot-hot all of a sudden. Face tingling. Him make a batting motion with his empty hand, unsure what to do with himself, his arms especially, they seem to just dangle stupidly by his side.

'Not that I'm a pro or anything. But if you want, I can teach you.'

'Really?'

The eyes shudder again. Lips pull back into an even wider grin. 'You know, I've always wanted to learn how to play. Most teams I join just didn't want beginners, though. It always puzzle me, how a man suppose to learn and get good, if nobody want when them green.'

Them walk out on to the field together, completely deserted by then, except for the two, and even night was setting up quick and brisk, with the sun already gone down and the evening starting to blow cold. Dale swing the bat this way and that, a skip in every step. The man, Nevin, beside him, calm, quiet. And for two months straight, thrice a week Nevin would come and them would practise on the field for two hours. During that time, Dale would show him how to hold the ball, how to position the wicket, how to

60

strangle the bat, underhand throws that would trick the opponent, special slides to use if him can't reach the wicket in time. Sometimes they would have practice runs and Nevin would curse and fling down the bat, annoyed that him couldn't hold it right, that him couldn't bat the ball properly, that every time him bowl, Dale would catch the ball expertly in his cupped hands.

After each game, sometimes them would rest under the willowy branches of a nearby guava tree and talk quietly as the sun slip from out the sky and hide behind the mountains, and swallows fly west for the night. And Dale would tell him about his Aunt Daisy who owned Rattler's cement factory with her husband, Mr Rattler, and how that was where him was living now since his mother passed. Him also worked there part-time. Dale would tell him too about his father who would drop by now and again but with whom Dale wouldn't exchange not even one word. But mostly Dale would listen, and watch the veins move up and down Nevin's forehead as him talk about his dog, Liver, that Mr Morgan did buy him at age ten, and that he'd kept for nineteen straight years until a mini-van knock her over one day as she was crossing the street. (She was blind in one eye and deaf in both ears.)

Then them would part for the evening and Dale would return home to his room at Aunt Daisy's, his face trembling with radiance some days, but cloudy on other days when him was certain Nevin didn't like him that way. But now and again, Nevin would invite him out to dinner, and during those times, Dale would be attentive and wide-eyed and quiet, admiring of the pleasantly dressed man sitting across the table from him, with the boyish gleam in his eyes, the velvet soft voice, that spoke so much about politics, but who, no matter how often and how hard him practise, would never be any good at cricket.

Other times him would talk about the days him used to travel all over the country, with Mr Morgan, who used to be a campaign manager for the Labor Party. Those days Nevin was bent on becoming district representative. Him did study political science at the University for several years, ran and lost in local elections three times, dropped out of the race altogether in the middle of the fourth election when Mrs Morgan push his father down the stairs crippling him for life.

Then one day the man ask if Dale would like to accompany him to the market where him keep a stall and meet his mother. And for several days Dale glowed, eager to meet the woman who had given birth to this man with the tremendous shoulders and dog-bite by his lips. The appointed evening Dale took a seat in the front of the pale yellow Datsun, his trousers smoothly ironed, his shoes brilliant from a fresh coat of polish. Inside the car, Nevin didn't speak much, him use one hand to guide the car, and the other to gently stroke the hair on his chin, in a tender, thoughtful way that made Dale think of his father.

'Think you'll go back into politics?' Dale break the quiet of the car.

'Probably not.' Nevin sigh long before him answer. 'Mrs Morgan ruined all that now. Hard to get back in, once you drop out. I don't know.' And him switch on the knob to the radio and all was silent again in the car, except for slow tunes oozing from the rear speakers.

Inside the market, the two walk briskly, embroidering their way pass vendors selling hairnet, scissors, comb, toothpaste, haircurler, razor blade. Them cry excuse, voices lost on the raucous hordes of people buying and selling and bargaining for low prices. It was Friday. Pay Day. Them duck under people's armpits, scale over tables and chairs, trespass through stalls until finally them arrive at a table that seemed to stretch for miles laden with rolls and rolls of fabric of assorted colours and prints.

'Mama, you ready to put up these things? This is Dale. Mama, you ready?' But Mrs Morgan didn't hear him. Her wide strong back was turned to them, her head tie-up with a turban made out of blue velvet, and she was arguing hard with a woman who wanted her to lower the price on a piece of fabric. Her big strong arms were akimbo and she rock back and forth on the balls of her heel.

'Then Miss May, if I give you this cloth for little and nothing, how I going to pay the rent end of month for this stall?' Her voice had the silver smoothness of Nevin's. It wasn't angry, just firm. She bend down to pick up several other pieces of fabric, run them through her finger. 'What about this one? Similar print. Here, feel it.' And she rub the heavy material against Miss May's hardened square jaw. 'Nice and soft, ain't it?' Miss May's hardened square jaw flinched. 'Mind you it's not cotton, but it's a little cheaper.'

But the woman was determined. She draw her face up into a tight line. She fronted her chest. 'Mrs Morgan, is a long time I been coming to you, you know. You know that is only me alone working since them lay off Egbert from the bauxite plant. If Egbert was working, you know I'd gladly . . .'

'Here, Miss May, take the fabric.' Nevin pick the cloth from out his mother's strong hands and begin to wrap it up in a piece of newspaper. 'Tell Mr Egbert howdy-do, for me.' Mrs Morgan's tea-coloured face didn't have on any expression, when she turn from Miss May to glance at her son. But Miss May's thin narrow face had lifted into a joyous smile.

'God bless you, Mr Nevin. God bless you, sir.' And she hurriedly grab the package with her short stumpy fingers, made a little curtsey and disappear through the crowd.

Dale was now left with the silence between Nevin and his mother. Whistling noisily Nevin start to roll up the fabrics and put them into boxes. Mrs Morgan was still standing up with her arms akimbo looking out at the busy market, her back turned to Dale same way. Dale clasp and unclasp his hands lying rigid at his side, uncertain where to put his eyes.

Slowly Mrs Morgan turn around and start to roll up the fabrics and put them into boxes. She still didn't acknowledge Dale standing in front the stall. 'When you going to get your own blasted stall, sir?'

'Mama, you know Miss May doesn't have the money . . .'

'I said, when you going to get your own blasted stall so you can run it your way.' Her voice was thunderous, her eyes flashing. From nearby, people pause to look.

Nevin kiss his teeth. 'Mama, this is Dale.'

Dale wanted to leave. His stomach was trembling. Him wasn't sure what to do with the expression on his face, if him should smile, appear serious.

'How are you, Dale?' She stretch out her hand, eyes solemn, voice still bitter.

Dale opt for the latter and pump her coarse, calloused hand

firmly. 'Hearty, thanks.' She looked nothing at all like Nevin, except for the eyes.

'Nice name.' She repeat it under her breath. 'I don't hear it often.'

Dale smile, and nod several times. 'Thanks.' Him could feel Nevin's eyes on the two of them.

Not long after them left. Dale sat in the back of the car and listen to the slow silent breathing of Nevin and his mother who didn't exchange one word during the course of the journey to Nevin's house. And them made love for the first, Nevin just as tender, just as sweet and as experienced as Dale had expected.

Dale look at Dr Barnaby. At the glasses perched quietly at the tip of her nose. At the swollen ankles pressed into her shoes. Him think about Johnney lean up against the column. Neck throw back, throat bare, brown, vulnerable to the white lights streaming out into the darkness. Him think about the circles that stay permanent around his own eyes these days, that no amount of castor-oil render scatheless; no amount of moisturising leave velvety. Hair no longer grow around the corners of his face. It recede from off his forehead stretching way back on to the middle of his head. Pimples spot his cheeks now, leaving them feeling rugged; lumpy; out of form; ugly.

'Must be him searching for a younger version of me.' Bitterness stained Dale's voice. 'Somebody fresh out of school. Ignorant. Eager. Another me four years ago. Like my father and mother all over again.'

'Yeah!' Dr Barnaby's moon face suddenly came alive, eyes darting around, voice restless.

'Must be him got tired of her. Them used to quarrel all the time. Mostly about the postmistress. She was younger. More sophisticated. She didn't have any children. Him used to go to her house every Sunday after church. Everybody in the district knew. Him didn't care.'

Dr Barnaby, her grey hair wrapped in a bun, nodded slowly, all the while looking at Dale, back bent slightly forward, size twelve feet folded uncomfortably at the fat ankles. 'It's tough, isn't it? Finding yourself trapped in the same position as your mother.

Cycle repeating itself. Only this time you're in the cog. Did your mother stay?'

Dale shake his head, sombre.

Dr Barnaby didn't say anything else after that. She put down her note pad and straighten out the pleats in her crisply ironed flowered skirt. End of hour was at hand. She adjust her bifocals and unfold her ankles. 'Come again next week so we can get to the root of this business.'

Dale never went back.

The coughing greet them first thing. Seeping out from underneath Ian's front door, it creep into the rubber soles of Dale's white sneakers, flutter the muscles in his stomach and cause an aching to rage crossway his back. Behind him, Nevin grunt-out nervous-like. Blow his nose inside the white, lace handkerchief and spit sudden. Tuck his shirt into his trousers, straighten his tie and run his hand quickly through his hair. Dale brace himself forward, head upright, knees firm. Together them step through the front door.

But by the time them settle inside the little studio, all signs of the coughing hang still behind the shades that cover over each window; lie dormant underneath the white lace tablecloth that flutter now and again from any slight wind movement; disappear sudden inside the dense green carpet that pad the floor.

Prop up against the bedhead, legs tangle-up inside the sheet, a copy of last week's *Gayly News* open wide on his lap, Ian's eyes follow as them come in, cigarette – lengthy with ashes – hang rakish from his mouth corner.

'You'd think with how sick you are, you'd have your Bible open-up instead.' Dale reach over and kiss his cheeks. Nevin straddle a chair far from them in the doorway of the kitchenette.

Ian shrug, cigarette steady in his mouth. 'Life have to go on, my love. Can't just give in.' Him pick up the magazine. 'A fellow in here sounds kind of interesting.' Eyelids squint down shut from the rising smoke, him read: 'Attractive, light-skinned, dentist, five-five seeks light-skinned professional type for friendship, possibly more. Send photo.'

65

'How're you feeling?' Nevin ask from across the room.

'Oh, just fine. Just fine.' Him knock ash into a nearby crystal tray, eyes steady on the magazine. 'Can't wait to get back to the office, can just imagine all the work on me desk. And that Roy is just absolutely useless. Cannot be left alone for long. Absolutely useless.' Him sigh, raise his head to glance at them, flash pearly white teeth, then return to the magazine on his lap.

'They give you medication?' Nevin again.

'Some stuff.' Ian frisk his fingers in several directions, annoyance strong in his gestures.

There was a long length of silence in the room, except for the soft rustling of the leaves as Ian turn the pages of the magazine, the humming of the refrigerator. Outside the rain had eased, yet thunder still rumbled intermittently. A little transistor on the shelf in the kitchen blurt out the time. Dale glance across the room at Nevin's stern profile, sitting rigid in the chair, legs crossed, hands clasp in his lap. Him wonder what Nevin had found in Ian, the four weeks them lasted. Ian was so frivolous, so light-hearted and gay, next to Nevin who was sort of stodgy and practical. Watching him sitting stiff in the chair, reminded Dale of the old cotton tree-stump that was behind the rabbit pen on his father's farm: weather-beaten, dry and strong.

'Ah!' Ian shriek from behind the papers. 'Listen to this one. Married English man seeks young native for discreet relationship.'

Dale grin. Nevin cough nervous.

One by one, Ian start to hand out the get-well cards spread out on the little dresser by his bed. Many were laminated with a sheet of plastic covering the outside salutation.

'That one's from John.'

Some of them Dale did see already. Him pass them on to Nevin across the other end of the room, who open them only briefly not bothering to read.

'That one's from Trevor. You member Trevor, Dale. The fellow who was hot after me for months.'

Dale nod, listening keenly. There was a certain shrill escaping Ian's voice now and again. Wasn't overly noticeable. For the most part you could overlook it, but every time it was about to emerge, burst forth, it slink back beneath a cackle of laughter, some new joke, a jab at somebody else.

'That one's from my mother.'

Dale look up at Ian, face confuse, then across the room at Nevin. Ian didn't return the gaze. Stretching his hand crossway the dresser, him knock ashes absently into a crystal tray. Then him hand Dale the bouquet.

Dale turn it over in his hand. The arrangement of twelve yellow roses. It didn't have a card attach. No handwriting with a little note. 'It's nice,' him say out loud, maybe too loud, trying to be cheerful, to conceal his surprise, slowly putting the bouquet to his nose, inhaling deep the scent from the blossoms before passing it on to Nevin.

'When she come see you?' All eyes turn back to Ian.

'Tuesday. She spend almost the whole two hours. We chat and laugh the whole time before them give me medication, knock me out.'

'You really think Miss Kaysen did come see him, Dale?' Nevin ask during the drive home, darkness masking them faces. It was raining again. The streets swimming with water. Deserted. Every few minutes the lightning struck, illuminating the car, a brilliant silver, outlining the expressions on faces.

Dale shrug, annoyed that Nevin should ask the very thing him was thinking. 'Why Ian must lie?'

'Just don't make sense. Not from what you tell me. But a mother is a mother. Must be she change her mind.' Nevin leave it at that and switch on the radio. The BeeGees.

But Dale wasn't quite through. Him think about the bags that hang underneath Ian's two eyes, the tiredness that seem to settle inside his face and press down the corners of his lips. The coughing that turn on and off as it have a mind, as it see fit for the occasion. The few minutes Nevin stepped outside to get his pipe from the car, the coughing exploded out of Ian like a clap of thunder, knocking him to one side of the king-size bed, rattling each saucer inside the cabinet, jangling every last one of Dale's nerve endings, leaving Ian ragged, crumple-over, slumped on to Dale's left shoulder when it finally passed.

Him signal to Dale for the medication him have stash underneath the bed, cover-up under two blankets and a set of pillowcases. Dale feed him the tablets, force the spoonfuls of syrup down his throat. Ian gasp. Him sputter. But not before Dale notice the specific times listed on the bottle. And that the last dosage was due half hour ago.

'Ian!'

But Ian already started up the hollering on Dale's left shoulder, and all Dale could do was to rub the head, badly in need of a trim, nestled on to his chest, and stroke his back in the places that didn't have much flesh, that stick out like shelves through the silk pyjama suit. Hold his hands that were cold and soft and without life.

'What them say wrong, Ian?' For maybe them tell him after all. Hand him the sheet of paper with the diagnosis write down.

Ian shake his head slow. 'Them don't know, Dale. Them don't know what cause the coughing. Why me can't keep down anything much anymore. Why the constant headaches.' Him start the crying again, not as heavy, but more whimpering, more like him afraid. Like him was seven again.

But the minute him hear Nevin rattling the door handle to come in, the second the door fly open, the tears slip way sudden, and the cheerfulness and laughter return.

'Nevin, please tell Mrs Morgan thanks very much for the lovely rum raisin cake she bake and send. Dale, you did get any? Best cake I ever behold. Melt right on your tongue.'

Dale did cry excuse and leave the room.

II

Dale didn't know exactly why him take the work, why him didn't go on and open the store with Nevin. Him know that anger was rooted somewhere in the decision, but then again, nothing atall comforted him more than to crochet table-top doilies and weave doorway mats; design and cut out patterns for clothes suiting any occasion. His mother would've been pleased. Was exactly what she would've wanted. And finally Dale own self would've had a foothold in the business, now him could meet Nevin on his own terms.

And it wasn't that all of a sudden Dale grew respect for Alexander; that what Alexander have to say, mattered; worth pondering over. But when Dale mention the conversation him did have with Nevin, one night while Alexander was driving him home, Alexander did outrightly say to him: 'You need to give Nevin a walk. You need to find your own work, find your own place. Live your own life, so you and him can see each other eye to eye. On the same level.'

'But it's different with a business,' Dale tell him, 'for then it'd be half and half. I would gain autonomy, independence.'

'Do what you want.' Alexander's Adam's apple bob slightly. 'But you need to shake that man. Give him a walk. Give him reason to respect you. Stay with him till you grey, and him still treat you like boy. I can get you a work at the post office.'

While Mrs Morgan claim she like how the uniform stretch crossway Dale's shoulders, stoutening him up, making him look more manly, Rose say she just cannot believe the complete air of authority that envelop him all of a sudden, bringing to mind when her man, Barry was in the army for several weeks. Nevin didn't have a word to say. A permanent scowl cast his face these days as if nothing atall titillate him, nothing atall can create little rhapsody in his life.

As much as Dale didn't like to acknowledge it, him couldn't help but enjoy the newness that overcome him every time him put on the postal service uniform. The big, heavy boots bring a welcoming security to his wide feet as him walk from one avenue to the next. Hands grow coarse from the constant rifling through paper, fingernails shorten, even his voice take on a certain hoarseness, gaze sharpness. Women turn to look again when him grunt out howdy-do. Men tip hats. Dogs yap at his heel and schoolchildren

69

run behind him. The uniform hug Dale's torso with a firmness so strong, it churn up a turbulence in his rump whenever him walk, thighs pummelling with each gait, boots grinding the asphalt, stirring up dust behind.

It frighten Nevin to no ends. Cause him to start dinner and set the table each evening him get home from work before Dale. Cause him to wash dishes now and again, to tidy the house, and help out with the laundry Saturday mornings.

But like Nevin, Dale know the moment him step out of the uniform, the minute him take off the hat and put down the badge, all signs of the confidence would drop way sudden. The chisels in his cheeks would fade out smooth; shoulders buckle forward again and his neck hang limp to one side. So him keep on the uniform all through the evening till late into the night when him finish studying and was ready for bed.

But Nevin did have the patience of Job. Waiting one night till Dale set up himself in his bed, him barge into the room, bringing with him a gale of ferociousness. Towering over Dale, hands fold crossway his barrel chest, him spit out: 'Thought you had more ambition than that.' The voice was bitter, scornful.

Dale's heart hammer inside his chest.

'Thought you wanted to make something of your life. You different from them others. But you ambitionless just like them.'

'A job is a job.' Dale didn't know where the calmness came from all of a sudden. 'As long as the means to getting the wages honest.'

'Frigging fool!' Spittle splash Dale's face. 'Owning your own business make a man out of you. Something you wouldn't know inside that damn stupid uniform. Working for somebody else is shit. You hear me, shit.' His voice ring hoarse into the stillness.

Dale didn't say anything. Nevin seem older these days, more tired. His moustache fit thick and heavy like a badge across his face.

'You get this shit job to spite me. To shame me in front my mother. In front my sister.' Him put his foot on the bed, jabbing Dale with the tip of his shoes. 'But you don't spite me Dale, you spite yourself. Blasted fool!'

But Dale didn't feel any of the hardness him see imprint inside Nevin's cold dark eyes. A soft laughter slide down into his belly instead, causing it to quiver. Him wanted to roar out loud at Nevin, before him, trembling with rage and something else Dale hadn't noticed in a while, hurt. For, no, him didn't like the job at the post office. It took time away from his studies; it was monotonous; it didn't pay anything much. Furthermore the presence of the uniform distanced Nevin. It took away the cuddling up at night ever so often; the smooching over the pot once in a blue moon as them prepare dinner; the tenderness that would come after each episode of love-making when them lie exhausted side-by-side talking into the early hours of the morning. And Dale missed it. But he'd been seeking ways and means to get back at Nevin, and accidentally he'd stumbled into it. In a chamber in his own castle, Nevin had lost the throne, in front of his mother, sister and invalid father.

Dale ended the relationship, not because he'd fallen out of love with Nevin as him led Nevin to believe or because him wanted an open relationship as Nevin assumed, but because it hurt too much to see Johnny's round dark face in the store around the counter making change give customer. And every time Johnny's deep coarse voice cackle into the receiver whenever Dale phone Nevin, it brought to mind pictures of the ice-pick and stirred up Dale's shame. And every time him came home from school wanting to cuddle up with Nevin, the house was usually empty, for Nevin would be working late as usual at the store as him go over accounts, count money, make plans, him and Johnny, head-to-head. Whenever a short school holiday presented itself, Dale would look forward again to the trips to some guest house or other, where the two could spend quiet times away from Mrs Morgan. But usually Nevin and the boy would be off to Brazil or Venezuela buying goods for his store.

And for twelve solid months, Dale bury his head in his Geography books, absorb his heart in Young People's Meeting, lock his eyes tight to the salvation taking place. And little by little him would find himself starting to pull away whenever Nevin reach over to touch him at night, complaining that him was tired, or stressed from an upcoming exam or paper. It even got to the point where every time Johnny's name was mentioned in the house; or whenever him would stop by the house to drop off a sample; go

71

over a travel itinerary; or to just say 'hello', a violent headache would suddenly overcome Dale leaving him paralysed.

But sometimes Dale would have someone take over for him at church, and him and Nevin would go away for several days. And after the initial days pass and Nevin finally feel confident that things were OK and him didn't have to call Johnney three times a day for assurance, then him would relax and Dale would catch glimpses of the Nevin him used to know, who still missed Liver, or who still can't play cricket or shoot marbles or whistle a tune, who sing off-key, and still liked to talk politics.

During those several days away, Dale's desire would return, but only if Nevin did not touch him. And at first Nevin liked the commands Dale would fling at him to undress and would often gladly comply, but when him finally came to terms with the added dimension, one long holiday weekend, Nevin held his head in his hands and wept for several hours. And after he'd blown his nose in his shirt several times and dry his eyes, Dale finally told him he wanted to see other people.

'OK.' Nevin's voice was as thin as a piece of paper. They were sitting inside the living room of a villa they'd rented for several days. Nevin was lying flat on his back, arms folded behind his head, in a long narrow straw couch. Dale was sitting up across from him in a stiff-back round wicker. The mouth of the thatched-roof hut look out at the heavy waves foaming and lashing violently at rocks.

The idea had only taken shape in Dale's head twelve hours ago, now it had grown permanent roots and was blossoming tremendously. It was too late to take it back now and most of all, him like the shadows of pain dancing back and forth across Nevin's face.

'Is it because I'm ten years older?' Nevin again, whispering.

Dale shrug, 'Maybe.' Inside his stomach was as hard as a piece of granite. 'Maybe.' Him sigh and make his way into the room where him start to pack up the suitcase. Out in the living room, Nevin continue to howl like a baby.

But it backfired on Dale, for not long after they'd returned to the apartment from the villa, a slew of fellows started coming and going from the house and at all hours of the night. But nonetheless, the hurt and pain that had danced across Nevin's face that afternoon was the very same one flickering back and forth on his face now as the tip of his shoes continue to jab Dale in his side.

Suddenly the laughter inside Dale's belly stilled, and the granite hardness returned, seeping over his eyes and tightening the corners of his lips. Dale spring up suddenly. 'Get your bloody foot from off the bed.'

Nevin's foot froze. Slowly him take it down and place it gently on the floor next to his other polished shoe.

'Get the hell out.'

Nevin hesitate. The anger had left his eyes. Fear replaced it. The centipede shivered.

'Don't you ever barge in here again without knocking. I was all set to move into that place on Webster Avenue but like the blinking idiot I sit down and allow you to talk me out of it.' (Of course, Dale didn't tell him how the idea of living alone in a one bedroom terrify him. How the idea of his mother sitting gently on his bed didn't bring him comfort, but terror.) 'This is my room. So respect that door. And furthermore,' Dale scream out to the retreating figure, back slump-down into his trousers, 'I'm under no obligation whatsoever to start a business with you.'

And with that Dale walk toward the door and slam it shut. Then him weep hot tears silently in his pillow for the remainder of night.

June 1978

I

Ian arrive at the restaurant late as usual, sweeping a sudden stillness over the room as him sway across the floor, arms akimbo, chest fling forward, the balloon-like proportions of his trousers swelling out around him. Pausing in mid-stride, neck slightly tilted, him glance quickly around the room in search of Dale, but long enough so all eyes could digest the perfect triangle of his bodice, the slender grace of his throat, the supple movement of his thin hips as him make his way over to Dale.

Hunched over the table in a corner, one hand holding up his jaw, the other swirling the straw in his glass of aerated water, Dale wait patiently, his back turned to the uniformed portrait of the Governor General. Him could see Ian approaching from out the corners of his eyes, but him didn't look up. Him didn't want to encourage it. And as if a sturdy handshake wouldn't do just as well, Ian stretch his entire length over the table to press wet kisses on either sides of Dale's bearded cheeks. Then him proceed to seat himself, first folding up the jacket so as not to unsettle any of the creases, then easing on to the very edge of the hard-back chair, legs gathered one on top the other, brows severely arched. Him snap for the waiter, bangles jangling.

'Aren't I just gorgeous?' him whisper at Dale, one hand patting the back of his head as if tucking into shape an elaborate coiffure.

Dale didn't say anything, merely grin with the edges of his face. For nothing at all about Ian looked good. His clothes hang off his thin frame like an old blanket. His jawbone jut out more than ever these days, pushing his eyes even further back into the sockets.

74

And his eyes didn't ripple the same kind of merriment like before, only a dull glow emanate from behind.

But Ian didn't care whether or not Dale plan to answer. Bending slightly forward, him peel down his shirt collar to expose a lumpy strip of purple easing its way across his throat.

'Love bites,' Ian assure Dale, plenty pride in his voice. 'Can't read or write, but cute everlasting.'

'Where'd you find him?' Dale ask, not certain him wanted to hear. Him could still feel a few stares bearing down at them.

Ian sigh long looking off at nothing in particular, hand with cigarette en route to his lips, poised high in mid-air. 'You going on as if tree growing in my face. As if I don't have charms and other delicious niceties.' Him knock ash into the tray and inhale deep.

Dale couldn't help but smile, wrinkles creasing the edges of his eyes, double-chin rippling smoothly. Just last week Ian wake up in time to find the fellow him bring home creeping out with the colour TV his mother return to him, untouched. 'How much money him take?'

'Three silk shirts me bring back from Canada last year and several ties me buy downtown. I even see him downtown in them. Have the nerves to walk past like him don't see me.'

'You call him?'

'Of course, me call him. Couldn't remember his name to save life, but might as well him service me for the two bow ties. Them cost a whole heap of money.'

'You mention the clothes?'

Ian shake his head, reaching inside his breast pocket for the spotless white handkerchief, initials embroidered in one corner. Him sop alongside his neck and daub over his face with quick light movements so as not to disturb the layer of powder. But not even powder could hide the pallor that was creeping into his collar, enveloping his entire person. Him take one sip of the soup the waiter bring, and push the rest towards Dale, complaining how restaurant food was tasting more and more like cardboard each day and if Dale didn't notice. When them get up to part, his shirt was sucking to his back like a second layer of skin, but him merely shrug it off, quickly pulling on the chequered jacket as if it

75

was common accord for someone to sweat like hog inside a fairly chilled, air-conditioned room.

Dale wasn't sure whether or not Ian was taking the medication the doctor prescribe to prevent the sweating. Him was afraid to ask, for fear Ian accuse him of interference, for his tongue was sharp, him know an abundance of hot words. Nevertheless, Dale couldn't help but wonder, especially when, several weeks back, Ian claim that the mother send him a vial-full of a potion to lessen the constant coughing. Dale didn't even bother to ask Ian to show the vial. Him didn't want to hear the elaborate story Ian would create, the intricate details him would get into. Dale only nod instead, his eyes springing water all of a sudden.

'It don't make sense,' Dale complain to Mrs Morgan, late one afternoon as him sip orange leaf tea from the couch in the office. She was standing up over her desk, studying the blueprint for a tunnel she plan to dig that would connect her house to Nevin's in case of Armageddon.

'First it was how the mother come to visit him in the hospital,' Dale continue on. 'And believe you me, Mrs Morgan, according to Ian's sister, the mother didn't put out her foot not even once. She didn't drop him not even one single solitary line. For she can't bear the sight of Ian. But nonetheless Ian was showing everybody the get-well card and the bouquet of flowers from Bennett's that him claim she send him.'

Dale pause, sighing loudly before slurping up a mouthful of the tea. 'Now him claim him not going to take the hospital medication anymore for the vial from his mother more than enough. Mrs Morgan, Ian don't have another friend as good to him as me. So, why him must constantly tell me untruths, I don't know.'

'Sounds like death might be stalking that boy, Dale.'

'Mam?' Dale look up, not quite sure how to read her. But her back, stiff and straight like a rake handle inside the brown frock, was in front him, so him couldn't see the grooves imprint on her forehead, the stillness in her eyes, the constant movement of her jaw, as her tongue roll back and forth the cap to a tube of cement glue; a ball of spit; a number-34-sized ball bearing or some such item from her toolbox under the desk.

'A dying man will grab at anything to give him peace, son.'

'Mrs Morgan, please don't talk damn nonsense.' Hoarseness overcome Dale's voice. 'Him younger than me you know. Kinder than Ian you can't find. If is the last penny him have, him would rather give it away and starve than . . .'

She spin around and look at Dale, jaw suddenly still, the funny left eye, mouse brown this morning to match her frock, not quite in focus on his face, but sliding pass instead, over his shoulders and on to the wall behind his head. 'You going on as if death usually ask permission before it visit. As if you can bargain with it not to come this week, but next month instead. To take John Brown's life instead of Mary Jane's.' She pause to swallow before continuing on. 'Some people blasted lucky. Them can smell it coming from all the way up the road.

'It give them time to pay back all the money them owe and confess which man's wife them used to sleep with. But other people not as strong. When death knock, them run and hide. Them laugh it off, build up stories around it. But you and I know that them only fooling themselves.' With that she turn back to her desk, jaw in full motion once again, the low tones of her mumble more pronounced.

The telegram arrive from the hospital not long after that, but Dale didn't have the gumption to read it. Him slip it on the kitchen table and walk pass it several times, eyeing it from different angles, bellying up enough pluck to finally tear it open. Him know from experience that telegrams don't bring good news. Only bad luck and other terrible things to come. Dale feel a buckling in his stomach. A familiar weakness that spread down into his knees, directing them forward and backward at the same time, like the day when the telegram arrived from the hospital where his mother was undergoing surgery for cancer.

Him was about fifteen then, his father was remarried to the postmistress and Aunt Daisy did come to take care of them. The messenger drop off the note first thing the Monday morning but Aunt Daisy couldn't bring herself to open it. Instead she send Dale up the road to call Mass Raffel to please come and open the telegram. Mass Raffel's reputation was well known the short time him relocate to the district.

That morning Mass Raffel kick off his black knee-high galoshes outside the doorway and wipe his feet several times on the mat, before stepping into the living room. Already a handful of people did settle themselves inside waiting. It didn't take long for the news that Miss Daisy get telegram to spread around the little district.

Without even turning the black of his eyes to glance at anyone in the room, Mass Raffel pick up the telegram between the remaining two fingers on his left hand. (People say him lose the other three fighting for England during the War.) Then with his right, him unhook the ratchet knife from his waist and flick it open with a quick swing of the wrist. The room held its breath as the blade, glimmering in the early morning sunlight, knife its way through the envelope, letting out soothing, silvery sounds.

Several women who'd come with babies fold over shoulders, wrap hands over the babies' mouths to stifle whatever holler would escape. Outside the engine of a car struggle to turn over – dead with each new start; a rooster trumpet out loud, then its screech as somebody dash a basin-full of half-dirty wash water after it.

With the same quick swing of the wrist, Mass Raffel close-up the knife, and without a word, drop the telegram on the dining room table and turn out through the door. Ten, eleven minutes pass, still not a soul moved, all eyes laid to rest on the little piece of paper, its edges fluttering back and forth in the early drifts of morning breeze.

Then like a gust of wind whipping through the room, a door slam shut and the crowd part itself down the middle as someone push them way up to the table, boots grinding into the concrete. It was Uncle Percy, the one who everybody whisper was 'that way'.

'You don't know that damn fool can't read, Daisy,' him bellow out to his sister, as him pick up the telegram, scanning it only briefly, before dropping it back on the table. 'Sister pass on last night while she under the anaesthesia.'

Dale pick up the telegram. It was from the same hospital them admit Ian last time. Him tear along the perforation, fingers fumbling slightly. If Nevin was home, him could read it first and then deliver the message secondhand with most of the sting gone from it. But the new fellow him pick up with these days cause him to be absent from the house two, three days at a time. Teeth clenched, eyes narrowed down to slits, Dale read the little note enclosed in the envelope. And without a sound, him put on his clothes and slip out the house.

The long neck girl at the reception desk didn't have Ian's name on her roster. She stare at Dale unsteadily, wanting him to leave so she can go to her other responsibilities. She glance at her long and polished nails. She click them repeatedly. She pause to sip water from a cup. She click.

Dale bristle, slapping down the telegram on the counter before her, scattering paperclips and sheets of paper. Him didn't give one blast about the pregnant mothers and elderly people sitting around in the waiting room, hands on jaws, face cover-over. 'How you mean, him's not here.'

With a slight scowl gathering around her forehead, the girl raise her dry head slowly, stretch her neck to glance at the note, then turn to check her files again, this time meeting Dale's gaze with hostility unfurling on her face. 'Oh, you mean the one them find in the park last night?'

'Beg pardon?' The hostility was just as strong in Dale's voice. Him hate the public hospital and the general ineptitude of everyone who work there with a perfect hatred.

'You know, Nanny Sharpe's.'

Silence crash through Dale's ears. Him swallow, unsure what to say to her, how to say it, what tone to use. Him wonder how them find Ian, what him was doing. Him could feel the girl's gaze on his face, her bright red lipstick lips curl-up, ready to fire, scorn in her big black eyes. 'Which ward you say him was on?' His own calmness catch him off balance, but him still couldn't bring himself to ask if Ian was all right, what happen to him this time, if it was the same business with the lungs or worse.

'12-B.'

She was still ready to confront him, to fight, but him walk off, hoping that nothing in his gait would reveal anything about him. Him was manly enough to pass. Didn't sport the same limp wrist cock off to the side as if about to express some great wonderment, or gentle sway of the pelvis thrust forward like Ian. The sleeves of his shirt weren't turned up in that way peculiar to fellows at the bar, showing off bulging, stone-like skin, his trousers weren't tight, pocketless, molding his buns into round pieces of hard dough bread. Him was barrel-chested, stocky around the middle, and walked with a confidence common to most married men. Furthermore, him was wearing man clothes today, dungarees, the heavy post office boots and a cap for it was drizzling outside. But him could still feel the words embellished on her brain, poised, ready to pounce from off her tongue.

Him couldn't believe Ian was still going to Nanny Sharpe's. Not after the doctor warn him against hackling the body. Not after what happen the last time. Several months back. Before the constant cough-cough and vomit-vomit; when Ian's face was still taut and darkness didn't circle his eyes; long before his mouth corners started tilting slightly downwards. Not long after them take a seat on the bench, its paint faded with age, and Ian light up a cigarette, a bull-doggish-looking fellow trudge pass, glancing at them only briefly, but long enough for Ian to put out the cigarette, and follow after.

Sit down on the bench alone, Dale wasn't quite sure what to do exactly. Him did promise to wait for Ian, but him didn't feel comfortable by himself. It was his first time. All around, trees stand up tall and weeds grow plenty. A foot beaten path trail off into the thickets. It was evening. Sun gone down for the day. Over in the main park, people walk dogs or stroll around with babies in prams. The 'KEEP OFF. NO ADMISSION THIS SIDE OF PARK' sign lay buried and trample-over not far from his feet.

Another man walk pass: fortyish, head bald completely, one foot slightly longer than the other. Him circle around since Dale didn't follow after and walk past again. This time slow enough so them could exchange howdy-dos. Dale leave before him come back around.

Later that evening when them meet up at Ian's place, a bluish bruise the size of a fist stained Ian's cheek. But him only shrug it off when Dale point to it.

'Ian, I don't mean to interfere in your prerogatives,' Dale start off tentatively, 'for you're your own big person, but sometimes you don't know is who you following into the bushes. Suppose is a straight man who hate people like us. Suppose is a ploy to get you into the bush so him can cut your throat, bust your head. Suppose is a police man. Suppose . . .'

'Lord, my love.' Ian fan his hand, annoyance strong in his voice, face furrowing up all of a sudden. 'You have to take chances. Can't just spend your life coop up inside the blasted house. You bound to start grow fungus. Furthermore you'd see the thighs on that boy? Joy unspeakable!' Him sigh long, entire body swooning with the release of air.

Dale didn't say anything. Him just continue to look on in silence, jaws slightly slack, vein twitching big in his throat. Him didn't like the carelessness to the tone, the reckless attitude, the fickleness of the response. But him hold his tongue.

Dale push open the swing door to 12-B. The smell of antiseptic and illness embrace him; causing him to stiffen in its clasps. Him glance around the room, rectangular in shape, several large windows spilling bright light on to the thirty beds crowded in, fifteen on either side, a corridor in between. Except for scratchy sounds ejecting from the overhead intercom now and again, the humming of a respirator tank, and light snores coming from one or two of the beds, the room was silent and yellow. Dale walk towards the sound of the respirator, steps heavy, uncertain. It was coming from one of the only three beds with the curtains pull shut around them. The telegram didn't specify any particular ailment. Only that Dale must please come, Ian admit again. Dale presume it was nothing more than the lungs falling in again like last time.

Dale pull open the first curtain, the cloth tight in his grasp, uncertain of what to expect. But him didn't recognise Ian any-where about. There was one person with the general length and shape of Ian but the face was different, too frigid, jaw too flat plastic-like against the soft fluffiness of the pillow.

Dale pull shut the curtain and start to tiptoe along the beds, looking at faces closely so as not to miss Ian. Him could feel his temper mounting again. No doubt the girl send him to the wrong ward with her inept self. Him kiss his teeth long and slow, well wanting to go up and trace her, but not having the heart, fearful of her hatred, her power over him, and then again this whole business with the park.

Somebody was waddling down the corridor towards him. A short, pot-bellied man swallowed-up inside the white smock and between a pair of stethoscopes. Wheezing kind of loud as if the walking was more than him could bear, the man shuffle up to Dale, peer at him over thick bifocals and extend his right hand.

Dale grab the hand, a wizened-up disfigurement, so small it could fit inside the mouth of a jar of Ovaltine.

'Walker.' The little hand pump Dale's hand. 'Dr Arnold Walker.' Then him slip it back inside the coat pocket, out of sight. Coffee stains dot the front of his coat.

'Relative?' The man start to walk off. The wheezing start up again.

'Ian? No. Friend. Him all right?' Dale follow after him, trying to keep abreast. 'Them say him was here. But . . .' Dale couldn't continue.

The man take his eyes off Dale and look far down the end of the corridor. His eyes shine a dull glow from underneath half grey bushy eyebrows. 'Them find him in the park, you know. Him go there often? Him one of them funny types? Where you know him from?'

Dale stare at the little man, hands clenched by his side. Two men in blue scrubs and hairnets breeze past with an empty stretcher between them, white shoes barely sounding on the concrete. Without much effort Dale could easily land his hands crossway the narrow little throat and squeeze it till nothing. Without much effort him could grab the head and ram it into the wall. Ram it till it crack open, everything pour out, slide down

82

into his neck, into his striped shirt collar, on to his chest, nastying up his white smock. Him didn't see what it matter; a sick man is a sick man. Why it should matter who him sleep with, where them find him?

Dale clear his throat, voice cold, dull. 'We attend the same church.'

The doctor look up at Dale, cocking his head so as to hear better.

'We teach Sunday School together,' Dale continue on, not certain where the gust was coming from all of a sudden. 'Going seven years now. Ebenezer Open Bible Church on Half Way Tree Road. 10.30–12 every Sunday. We preach from the Old Testament, sometimes the New.'

The doctor fan his hand.

'What happen to him?' Dale ask again. 'The girl at the counter say him was here, but I don't see him. Him all right? I got the telegram this morning and came first thing. What happen to him?' Dale's voice was beginning to rise.

The little hand whip out a pink serviette and mop the doctor's face. 'We like to know a little something about our patients. That's all. Him in church. Good.' Him nod, several times before starting up again, voice soft, tones low. 'We going to operate this evening and see what we can do. Bad seizure him have in the park. Maybe something out there upset him and bring it on.'

'What you mean, seizure? What you mean?' Dale ask, voice becoming more and more loud as him follow after the doctor, back towards the beds. The same beds with the blue curtains pull shut.

'Him not down there,' Dale pull his shoulders. 'I already checked. Him not there.'

The doctor stop. Him turn to Dale, face stern, eyes hard. 'Look, you have to be strong, you hear me. You can't carry on like this. Fenky-fenky-like. Ian hasn't seen the face yet. Him say it feel stiff, but him unconscious mostly. So . . .'

'What happen to his face?' Dale whisper, rigid all of a sudden, chest braced slightly forward.

II

Outside the iron studded gates of the hospital, the paper bag with Ian's clothes clutch tight underneath his arms, Dale cross the street, heading north towards Constance Spring Road. The rain had eased, and heat simmered off the asphalt. Cars roar pass, buses too, but Dale didn't raise his head once to see if him recognise anyone along the tree-lined roadway. Shoulders drooped, one hand tucked tight into front pocket of jeans, Dale trudge on, eyes paying attention to nothing in particular, nostrils picking up now and again the mingled scents of melted tar, Esso gasoline, jerk pork.

The thought of going back to the house didn't sit easy with him. These days just the sight of Nevin's car pull up in the carport always leave him fearful. For him didn't know if that is the day him going to find his books pack up neat, greeting him in the doorway of the study, all his mother's dead-left figurines sweep in a puddle, providing more room for the new fellow to move in with ease. But usually it's Nevin alone perch-up on the couch with a Louis L'Amour or newspaper in hand, face up close to the text, glasses in arms reach; or standing half naked by the closet door as him sort through clothes to put inside the overnight bag lying empty on the bed.

Sometimes while en route to his own little room further down the hall, Dale would suddenly stop, seized by a slice of sun splashing across Nevin's face from a nearby window, illuminating the scar by his mouth. Watching from the doorway, blind to the chest of drawers lean-up against the wall, a pair of socks, roll-up, tossed careless on the floor, floral curtains waltzing to slight wind movement, Dale's eyes would drink in the tufts of hair crowning rigid nipples that heave up and down with each intake of breath. Protruding navel. Full imprint braced against black briefs.

And all of a sudden Dale would feel his own stomach muscles tightening, his own breathing picking up in pace, a gathering in the small of his back, a thickening in the root. And immediately him want to approach Nevin: one hand twisted lovingly around the noble throat, gently bending back the head so him can shove tongue deep inside Nevin's mouth; the other hand thrust down inside Nevin's pantry, hungrily hunting around in the darkness, groping, kneading, stroking the already hardening flesh; oblivious to the slight gasp that escape velvet lips, the confusion blanching Nevin's face.

But Dale know better, him know that the best thing is not even to turn the corners of his eyes and seek out temptation, but just to continue on pass the door and down the passageway. For there wouldn't be any tenderness in Nevin's eyes when him pull Dale face-down on the bed and ease off his trousers, tugging with the buttons, buckle clinking. All that was gone now. Only a dull hardness would settle itelf in the crux of his jaw, a stillness guarding his eyes. Upon completion, Nevin would simply haul back on his briefs, lips quivering slightly, and continue to fold clothes neatly into the overnight bag, while Dale remain tangled inside percale sheets, face flat amongst the folds of the pillow.

At the intersection, Dale wait with another woman, the hem of whose pale yellow frock was pulling out at the back, for the lights to change. A broad-shouldered fellow in shorts ride pass on bicycle, marble calves shuddering with each pedal. Dale turn right on to Exodus Lane. A nightclub was nearby. Maybe him would just stop in for a spell, punch a few tunes on the jukebox, sit up by the bar and sip an aerated water. If Nevin wasn't home then the house would be empty with only the creaks from Mr Morgan's wheelchair to listen to, as it roll from one end of the carport to another, or Ian's voice swelling in his ears, ejecting garbled sounds that grate Dale's nerves.

The doctor did bring Dale back to his office, an L-shaped little room with a skylight and coloured charts on the walls. Him wave Dale into a chair and take his seat at the untidy desk, sorting through a folder Dale imagine must be Ian's file. Him thumb through the notes muttering to himself, pausing to lick his forefinger at each page.

'It's high blood pressure that cause the stroke.'

'And nobody could see that it was rising.' Dale feel himself bridling again. Scorn filled his voice. 'All the time him been coming, nobody competent enough to monitor it.'

The doctor take off the bifocals and wipe his eyes with the tail of his smock. 'Let me show you something.' Him beckon to Dale, adjusting the wings of his glasses around elf-like ears.

Leaning over, Dale's eyes follow the stubby little finger along the lines of a chart. His hair smelled of coconut oil. His clothes, Brut.

'The blood pressure was regular. Has always been regular. Even when him was spitting out blood.' Pause. 'This here is new development.' Him jab at the number on the chart with his finger. There was silence again. Scratches from the intercom.

Dale sigh and straighten his shoulders. The doctor, easing back into the chair, put down the folder on the desk and turn to him. Him pass his tongue slowly over his lips. Readjust the glasses that had tipped down to his nostrils.

'I know this might sound funny . . .' Here him pause to scratch underneath his chin, to cup his jaw as if a case of toothache had suddenly come on. 'There was a man here named George Brookes with the same symptoms. Same coughing. Same spitting up of blood. Same . . .'

'Yes? And?'

'Slip into a coma two weeks ago.'

Silence resonate in the room for a while. Dale concentrate on the steel toe tips of his shiny black boots. Him didn't hear the phone ring. Nor the doctor's muffled tones inside the receiver. Didn't hear the slam of the file cabinet or the shuffling of papers as the doctor refiled the folder.

Them did walk back slowly along the corridor towards Ian's bed. Him was awake now, a nurse lady in attendance. For one brief second, Ian's eyes brighten in recognition before settling back into their gel of haze. Then as if something suddenly occurred to him, him start to gesture wildly, fingers stiff, mechanical, eyes watery, shifting around restlessly in the porcelain face.

But Dale couldn't spell sense of the uneven gestures Ian was making with his hands, mostly circular motions around the legs. Bending closer, Dale try to shape the words him imagine were escaping rigid lips. Him could figure out the 'Don't', but that was all. Confused, Dale did turn to look at the doctor, quiet by his side, for explanation, but not before Ian's screech spin him back around. The doctor fish a Bic from out his pocket and hand his clipboard to Ian. 'Write it down,' him cry out. 'Try and write . . .' But with one quick jerk, Ian only box the pad one-side and turn his face to the wall.

There was a thin, yellow fellow slouched-over at the bar when Dale step inside, elaborate swirls and rings from his cigarette dancing like angels out of his hair. Him didn't turn to glance when Dale drop off the paper bag a few stools over and head towards the jukebox, him remain hunched over his drink, shoulders broad, round, the outlines of his face hidden in shadow. Except for the grey-haired man playing chess with bartender at other end of counter, the bar was empty. Cracks peep out from the red concrete. Cigarette burns dot the green plastic covers of every other stool.

With slow tunes now piercing the quiet, Dale take a seat at the bar, slap a few coins on the counter, beckoning the bartender. Him wouldn't stay long. Just one drink. There was a Geography paper to attend to. Bill to get in touch with, and Ian's sister. Him was through with Miss Kaysen. The man was staring. Dale could feel the eyes steadfast on his cheeks. Now roving up and down his neck. Now along the sides of his face.

Absently Dale turn to meet the gaze. And for one quick second his heart stop, then start up again. His eyes darken, before brightening. Much thinner. Even taller. With a lemony complexion instead of Nevin's chocolate brown, but that was the only difference. He had the deep-set eyes, same cleft to the chin, same grin lurking around the creases of his eyes, before flaring out his nostrils and widening his lips like Nevin's. And as if his legs had suddenly developed power, them slip down off the stool and head over to the man, for all Dale could see was Nevin in the man's eyes, in his laugh, in his teeth.

The fellow had ceased blowing rings by now and was flicking ash repeatedly in his tray, grin frozen on his lips.

Up close, Dale paused. Maybe him should put more coins in the jukebox. Maybe him should just pass the man and continue on till him reach outside.

'Want a drink?' Dale's voice was almost a whisper. The bartender was upon them.

'No.' Even the voice was the same deep bass like Nevin's; scent of his breath vigorous from stale tobacco and gin; front teeth slightly overlapped, kissing. Dale order his own.

'You should come home with me.' It wasn't a question, more like a basic fact of life.

'Beg your pardon?' Dale clear his throat. The man's middle finger was tapping gently to the music, abandoned cigarette burning on its own. 'Now?' Dale's heart race. Him didn't even know this man from Adam. Didn't shower or anything this morning.

The man stub his cigarette and hop off his stool. Keys jingle from inside trousers pocket. Him look quizzically at Dale.

This was the very same thing him been cautioning Ian against. But it was starting to feel so exciting. For ever since Alexander explain that them might have to cool it for a while, the wife was getting suspicious and threatening to leave, there hadn't been anyone. Going two months now. But here was somebody who him could have pressing engagements with again. In the middle of another fight with Nevin, him could just get dressed and dash-off. Here was someone whose gifts him can drop careless around the house for Nevin to notice. And without even waiting for the bartender to return with the drink, Dale grab the paper bag with Ian's trousers and follow briskly behind the fellow to the car outside.

Much later, in the dead stillness of night, when Dale wake-up to a pressure on his arm and a lone dog barking from somewhere close, his mind run immediately to Ian and him bolt upright on the bed, finally understanding what Ian must have been saying. The gestures were to his feet, the paralysed legs. 'Don't mention it to anybody,' him was trying to say.

Glimpses of the past few hours rush into Dale's head. Overcome by a brief spurt of love, him turn to Loxley snoring gently beside him, lips slightly ajar, perfuming the already heat-oppressed dark with the mingled scents of decaying teeth, stale cigarette, gin. Dale bent to lick the cheek bones jutting out in the darkness, the square chin. His tongue settle in the cleft before meandering down to the throat and hardened chest. It linger there for a while, parting strands of tightly curled hair, listening for the faint heart beat. Him was five years older than Dale and nothing at all like Nevin. Him lack the grace, the charm, the poise, the intelligence. Him reminded Dale of a younger version of himself; politically uninformed, inexperienced, trivial. And him despised it. Silently Dale jump out the bed, put on his clothes, pick up the paper bag and slip out the house.

Not long after, Dale move in with Loxley. Not because him was in love, but because every time him would wake up sobbing in the middle of the night, choking sobs that echo throughout the small low-ceilinged apartment, Loxley would never ask a question, merely hug Dale close in his long slender arms, rocking him gently, telling him over and over it's all right, till the sobbing subside and the two of them could drop off to sleep again. The sex didn't cause dogs to bark or branches to shake, but given the circumstances, it would suffice for the time being.

Loxley hire a van and Dale pull up at Nevin's house early the Tuesday morning to collect his things. Him was hoping that no one would be home, but that was the very day Mrs Morgan chose to get her annual check-up instead of going to the market, and by 11 had already returned and was outside measuring and marking the foundation for the underground tunnel. The wide expanse of her strong back bending over was facing Dale as him step through the gate. She didn't stop to straighten. Only the sound of her voice raking up to Dale break the quiet.

'You going?'

'Yes.' Dale's voice was calm. 'I waited too damn long.'

'You chatting big now.'

Dale didn't say anything. Him swallow slowly, eyes blurry all of a sudden. Behind the house, under the mango tree, low guttural tunes squeezed-out from the bottom of Rose's belly pervade the morning. The Rastafarian, Barry, was strumming on his guitar. Mrs Morgan was speaking again. Dale turn back to her, clad in an old pair of Mr Morgan's khaki trousers and a sleeveless grey shirt.

'Maybe you should give him another chance.'

'Not over my dead body.'

'Then I guess we just have to wait and watch.' With that she pick up her pipe that was lying nearby, and continue to hum along with the tune oozing out from behind the house. Dale swallow again and start off towards the house.

By 2 o'clock, Dale did have everything pack up neat in the van. Over the weeks, little by little, he'd been preparing; packing up bags of clothes, his mother's dead-left curtains, enamel mugs, bath towels, curtain rods, tablecloths, china; not atall certain when the day would finally show itself. The larger pieces of furniture, like his desk, few lamps, three chairs, him beg Barry to help him carry. It was the first time he'd ever been in a room close-up with Barry. Him wear long dreads that spill down his shoulder and across his back like thick pieces of frayed rope; and him exude the scent of ganja so strong, Dale did have to open-up several windows so as not to become intoxicated. Back and forth from the house to the car, them load and unload furniture, Rose watching from the house corner, arms akimbo, a green cloth wrap around her hair; Mrs Morgan's strong firm back turned toward him same way.

Bill buy Ian a handsome leather chair with padded arms and a headrest and wheel Ian home from the hospital. Each time Dale visit, all that greet him is a pair of eyes, the colour of curry, sitting inside the darkness, shoulders slumped down into his belly. His entire left side was as stiff as a piece of board. Nothing atall moved, except for the rolling of his eyeballs, an occasional bobbing of the Adam's apple. Drops of saliva curdle themselves by the edges of his mouth.

Him use one cigarette light another, stretching and twisting the fingers on his right hand, and only sighs escape his lips. Huge, heavy sighs that hang still and permanent in the smoke-filled dark. Ian whose laughs, whose loud melodious rings used to swirl from one corner of the apartment to the other, were no more. Each time Dale open the window to let in fresh air, Ian scream from his chair to slam it shut. Each time Dale try and hang a bright new curtain, Ian reach over and rip it down with his good hand. Once a week,

Ian's little sister, Andrea, shave his face and trim his hair, alarmed each time by the thick clumps that stick to the comb teeth every time she run it through his hair. Every two weeks, the older brother Courtney send a money order to help pay for groceries, but not once did he put out his foot to visit. Neither the mother.

Bill hire a stout little woman named Dimple Biggs to come in and care for Ian. With the most colourful velvet turbans tying up her head, each morning bright and early, Miss Dimple rock and hum her way through the gate, a brown denim jacket fold up neat over her arm, a blue cellophane bag underneath containing her thermos full of cerosee tea, a large black Bible eaten up around the edges and a few pamphlets tie together with a piece of elastic. She set herself down on the verandah, black frock lapped between her knees, and sip-sip her tea while reciting passages till 7 o'clock approach when she let herself into the house.

Once inside, she set down her bag on the floor of the closet, slip on her house slippers, straighten out her dress and sing out from the foot of the stairs: 'Mr Kaysen, ready for your shower, sir?' There was a bell within reach of Ian's right hand on the small dresser by the bed. This him would ring in response to Miss Dimple's calls, or whenever him need assistance. Then she would make her way up the wooden stairs, humming softly under her breath, knock timidly at the door before entering to lift Ian from out the bed, set him gently on to the chair and wheel him into the bathroom. There she would lift him from the chair again and set him up on a little wooden bench already sitting inside the tub. The first two weeks him used to scream at her to leave, embarrassed at having to expose so much helplessness. Little by little him start to bend.

Each evening after Miss Dimple latch on his diaper and leave, Dale stay with Ian till him fall asleep or till Bill come. Sometimes them play Ludo, Hangman, cards, Dale pausing now and again to wipe the spit falling from Ian's mouth corners with a white towel. Other times Dale read to him poems from Bennett's collections in dialect or orate a scene from one of Walcott's plays. One night Dale strum a few tunes him remember from music lessons on an old guitar badly in need of tuning him find in the cellar of Ian's apartment. But Ian tell him to put it back in the closet and not to interfere with it again. Apparently it belonged to Ian's father who used to play in a folk band. But sometimes Dale would come and when Ian's face wasn't turned to the wall where no amount of coercing would bring him around, him cry silent tears that would often build up in his throat bringing on fits of coughing.

It wasn't often that him run into people him take a sudden dislike to. Especially women. But Dale didn't like Miss Dimple. Maybe it was because of the way she walk so quiet around the house that one could never really tell the exact moment she step into a room and begin to dust. Maybe because she'd never look you straight in the face. Her eyes were always focused on the dent at the base of your throat, your earlobe, tip of your forehead, or whatever else of interest going on behind your back. Sometimes while upstairs reading from a collection of Salkey's short stories, him would always feel as if she was listening from somewhere close disapprovingly, even though him could still hear her downstairs panker-pankering in the kitchen.

'Where you know her from?' Dale couldn't help but ask Bill one afternoon them run into one another. Bill was bringing in groceries, both hands full. Dale was just leaving. Dale follow him back into the apartment. Miss Dimple had already left. Ian was upstairs sleeping.

'Friend of a friend.' Bill put down both bags on the counter and start to stock tins on shelves. 'She use to take care of his mother, something like that.' Him pause to light a cigarette. Dale wonder what was between him and Ian. Why him continue to put in the extra time; to care for Ian. Was it because, like Dale, him too feel sorry for Ian or was it something else on his agenda, altogether. 'She working out OK?'

'Yeah.' Dale smile nervously, unsure whether to mention the 'Put your trust in Jehovah' pamphlets him would sometimes find underneath Ian's pillow, between the folds of his sheet, paste up on the dresser. All day long she play and replay the same religious tunes and Billy Graham's Sunday broadcast, as if trying to deliver a special message to Ian. Him even overhear her reciting Ian's name to God during her many daily incantations. Not that there was anything wrong with that, for even him, self, offered Ian's name to God in many of his prayers. But it was the fervour with which she would practise it, sometimes six and seven times a day, as if she expected an instant miracle. 'Just that she doesn't speak much. Is a little uncomfortable to be around her, sometimes.' Bill was staring, cigarette hung askew from pursed lips, eyes squeezed shut from the rising smoke. Dale bend to scratch an imaginary itch below his knee.

Silence ensue them.

Dale wonder if Bill know about the letters. Ian's letters to the mother, typed and in chronological order, underneath the bed inside an old blue plastic folder, Dale come up on accidentally. Letters expressing thanks for various gifts the mother send. Other ones making references to certain conversations and meetings they had on specific dates. None of them true. All imaginary events.

'How things going with that fellow you live with?' Bill break the silence, adjusting his broad floral tie over plain white shirt and high-rised gut.

'We not together anymore.'

'Oh!' His smile was charming, it sparkle his eyes and cause his brows to quiver. 'That means you're on the market again?'

Dale smile, unsure how to respond. Him wasn't sure what Bill meant, exactly. On the market for whom? All of a sudden Dale didn't like his teeth. His grin like a fox. But same time Ian started to cough and with a cry of excuse, Dale head off towards the stairs. Him wonder if Ian was listening.

'Maybe we can have a meal together.'

Halfway up the stairs, Dale turn to look down. Bill's eyes were bright hazel.

'Have another trip tomorrow. But maybe when I get back.'

Dale nod and carry on up the stairs.

The room Loxley offer Dale as study overlook a nursery where small children, in a flurry of chequered skirts and khaki shorts, play ball in the yard and shriek gaily all day. Dale didn't mind, sometimes him hang his head out the window and watched, following the game at first, before drifting off. Him wasn't sure if moving there was the right thing. Him didn't know how long him would stay; how long this fly-by-night romance between him and

Loxley would last. When Loxley offer him the place, at first him did say no. For certainly Loxley was joking. But Loxley's eyes that look so much like Nevin's dirt-brown ones were sombre, and the grin had disappeared from around his chubby lips, and Dale knew him was serious. And suddenly Dale felt anxious, for it felt like the beginning of another marriage. But must be Loxley sensed it, for him touch Dale's soft hands with his own and tell him to just try it for awhile. No obligation to stay.

Still Dale wasn't sure. Him'd only known Loxley now ten days total. But at nights as him lay down quiet on his cot in Nevin's house, him like more and more the idea. Ever since the incident that night with Nevin in his room, the amount of fellows coming and going from the house and from Nevin's room had multiplied. Sometimes Dale run into them coming out of the bathroom while on his way in, sometimes them brush against him at the gate. Some Dale knew, others him wasn't atall familiar with. Sometimes several came in one evening at different intervals. And to all of this Dale locked his eyes.

Dale wasn't sure what Nevin say to Mrs Morgan or if them discuss it any atall. But from Mrs Morgan him sense an air of chillness, so him put off meeting her on Sunday mornings for breakfast and ended the early morning walks to meet the bus. At church Dale enrol for several more sections of Bible study and Sunday school, and busy himself with school. And so when Nevin open the second haberdashery store and hire one of the fellows Dale ran into *en route* to the bathroom to manage it, Dale didn't allow Loxley to ask a second time. Him hastily put relocation plans into action.

Those mornings when Dale didn't have classes, him unpack his photographs and fountain-pen collection, his jars of assorted sizes and colours and arrange and rearrange the furniture in the apartment sometimes to the point of dizziness. After work, him scurry home quick so him can have Loxley's dinner ready. But sometimes Loxley would already have dinner on the table; other times him take Dale out to eat, always to places where Dale hope him would buck up into Nevin, if not into their mutual friends.

Every other Sunday Dale accompany Loxley on the three-hour train ride to visit his parents who live way up in Blue Mountains where snow sometimes cap the highest ridges, depending on the intensity of the cold front blowing down from Canada. The little white house sat like a great sentinel on top of a hill overlooking the surrounding district. Seven black, waist-high, sharp-teethed German shepherds guard the gate, and not even Loxley can walk through unless his mother, a squat, big-bosomed, round-faced lady, call them each by name, scold then speak kindly, before chaining them up.

Every Sunday them visit, the mother's wig was always neatly ironed and curled, her face powdered and her brooch hitched to her chest as if expecting stranger. Once around the dining table, lay out with her best pieces of china, she would serve Loxley the finest cut of meat, wait with her heart galloping in her chest to see if him like it, before moving on to serve the father – an older and solemn version of Loxley who always wear a brown suit with a rose from the garden outside on his lapel, and who frequently clean his throat as if phlegm constantly lodge itself there – then to Dale and finally herself. Every opportunity she get, she reach up to straighten Loxley's collar, to brush fuzz from out of his hair, or to bend down pick lint from off his trousers.

Inside the house pictures of Loxley during various stages of development bedeck the walls. And on top of the television set in the drawing-room, a portrait of the policeman Loxley lived with for ten years before him was shot in action stand guard.

'. . . Was a nice-nice man,' the mother did tell Dale, plenty pride in her voice, as she lock Dale's arms in hers and lead him on a grand tour through the old house and outside into the garden, the first time Dale visited. 'Him and Mr Hunt used to shoot rabbits every Saturday morning and just very, very caring to Loxley. So much better than that other fool Loxley used to go out with.' She pause to shake her head, lips wire-thin. Dale didn't quite know what to say, how to act, her openness catch him off balance. Furthermore, Loxley don't really mention the policeman much. Sometimes Dale would search through the drawers of his desk for a photo, but nothing. After the death, Loxley did move out of the apartment them used to share, leaving behind all physical traces of that part of his life.

At night, with Loxley's head neatly tucked underneath Dale's arms, fast asleep, chest rattling peaceful, Dale would still be wide awake, eyes turned to the ceiling, cold sheets soaked with sweat pull up to his neck. Him was afraid to shut his eyes. The same dreams haunt him each night. Dreams about his mother's funeral. But every time him look in the casket, it was Ian's face that stare back at him, one half smooth and stiff like a piece of china, the other half tender with the laugh lines spreading like branches around his mouth.

And in the early morning hours, when Dale would awaken to the sounds of Loxley's chest rattling out the same 'ke-hem ke-hem' accompanied by a mouthful of purple phlegm like Ian's, him didn't even stop for a second to contemplate that this might be the same disease plaguing Ian. Him merely roll out of the bed and amble quietly into the kitchen where him press limes on the white Formica counter to soften them, then squeeze them into a big tumbler filled with castor oil and feed it to Loxley, one slender spoonful at a time.

Nevin left a handwritten note at the post office, telling Dale to please meet him at Tulanes' for lunch, Thursday at two. Several times that morning Dale used the call-box out front and phone Nevin's place of business to cancel. But each time Johnney's voice cackle into the receiver, Dale hang up sudden. Him refuse to even exchange as much as two words total with that man. Going three years now. Furthermore, Nevin was the last person him wanted to see right now. For two weeks him been busying himself with school, end of term exams, final papers. For two weeks him been absorbing himself with Loxley, making brutal love to him the minute images of Nevin flash through his mind.

For two weeks him been wracking his brains, trying to figure out how to continue school next term, from whom him could borrow money. His own savings had dwindled down to nothing, for him insist on buying food since Loxley won't allow him to pay rent. Whenever Loxley bring up the issue, Dale slap it one side. Him couldn't take money from Loxley, it was bad enough to be living there, knowing full well him could never fall in love with Loxley. His poor mother would stir in her grave if Dale did ever take the money. Spurred by desperation however, Dale did make his way over to his Aunt Daisy's. She was glad to see him, but Mr

Rattler, as if knowing exactly why Dale come, wasn't exactly jocular. Him shake Dale's hand and let out his familiar boom-boom laugh, but his eyes didn't soften.

'Hard times these, Dale,' Aunt Daisy tell him as she lift up the trapdoor underneath her bed and feel for the box with the revolver and her money bag. 'The cement not selling. People not making houses like before. Sorry to hear that you lose the scholarship the school was offering.' She pause to count the dollars fold up neat inside the red handkerchief, lips moving slightly, her face sweaty, bearing strong resemblances to his mother's. She thrust half towards Dale. 'This is all I can spare, Dale. Hard times, these.' Dale did take the money and leave. It still wasn't enough, but it was a start.

When Dale finally arrived at Tulanes', twenty minutes later than agreed, after changing and rechanging his mind several times, Nevin was already seated at the table nearest the fountain, sipping a cold RedStripe, the air around him calm, confident, as if well aware that Dale would come. Him was wearing a blue and white chequered shirt Dale didn't recognise and had shaved off his moustache. Him look younger, Dale thought.

There was a Woolworth's bag on the seat next to him. Him glance up just as Dale approach and smiled. Dale's heart whipped up in pace. All the love rush back into his stomach. Hardening himself, him inhale deep and Dale take the seat Nevin gallantly leap up to offer. A drink was already poured and waiting.

'Some letters and things came.' Him hand Dale the plastic bag.

'How thoughtful,' Dale add, much too brightly, glancing at the cards from friends, a letter from his French pen-pal. Him couldn't decipher Nevin's mood.

'Oh, by the way, Rose and Barry getting married. She ask me to get your address so she can send you invitation.'

Dale smile to himself and look pass Nevin's shoulders to the couple behind. Several other tables were occupied. Waitresses in white shorts suits scurry back and forth with trays held high. Him wonder if it was really Rose who wanted the address. 'She can send it to the post office.'

Nevin didn't say anything. Him sip more of his beer.

Two dogs play close by. A baby girl scamper by, arms outstretched, legs stiff. The overweight father shuffle after, making cooing sounds.

'You happy, Dale?'

'Excuse me?' Irritation stained Dale's voice.

'I mean, with the new fellow.'

'Very happy.' Dale wasn't sure if his tone was convincing. Him glance at Nevin's finger, drawing circles on the table with the sweat from his beer. Him was still wearing the ring they'd exchanged. It gleamed mockingly at Dale. (Dale had buried his in the plot of land in front the house the same day Nevin hired Johnney to run the store.)

'I hear him look a little like me.'

Dale laugh out (perhaps a little too raucous) and shake his head, no merriment at all in his eyes. 'Don't flatter yourself.'

Nevin shrug. 'That's what I hear.'

The little baby scamper past again, fat man bringing up the rear. Dale did drag Loxley to the bar the Saturday night. It was nice at first. Him parade pass Nevin's friends, eyes elsewhere, with Loxley in tow. They'd danced to almost every tune, fingers touching. But as it got later and later and still Nevin didn't show, suddenly the music became too jarring, and Loxley's arms draped crossway Dale's shoulder, started feeling more and more like a great big burden.

'Anyway, so why you want to see me?' Dale raise his head to look at Nevin directly, eyes massaging square jaw, puckered lips, before laying to rest at the jugular beating steady in his neck.

'Well,' Nevin's eyes narrowed. Hands start to flail around. 'I come home one evening and the house empty. All your things gone. No note. Nothing. Mrs Morgan claim you say it finished. What about our relationship? What about your school fee? I promised . . .'

'You don't have to pay it anymore.' Dale's voice was still, eyes trembling. 'I making more money now. I can take care of myself.'

'Nonsense!' Nevin grab a blank cheque from out breast pocket and shove it towards Dale's, eyes brilliant.

'I don't need charity.' Dale's voice was beginning to stretch.

'Nonsense!'

'Can't bear to not have me draped around your little finger, can you?'

'What?'

'Can't bear to have me gone, huh?'

'Oh, Dale. Don't be fucking childish. I made a promise . . .'

'Well, this is what you can do with your fucking promises.' And in one quick flash, Dale pick up the cheque in his palm, crush it into a small ball and send it sailing into the waterfall. It danced amidst the sprays, hopping this way and that, before disintegrating into soggy white shreds. The little girl scuttle pass again, screeching out loud, the daddy, out of breath, struggling behind.

Mid-July 1978

At 2.30 every afternoon, Miss Dimple would waltz her way up the stairs as usual, her floral skirts shuffling out around her bow legs, and knock boldly at Ian's door before stepping inside to raise him off the bed and on to the wheelchair. (Once she did barge in unannounced, and Ian fling the metal ashtray towards her head, missing her forehead by a few degrees.)

One Thursday afternoon, however, after knocking several times and still no answer, she did barge in, her heart galloping in her bosom, the charcoal pupils of her eyes staring wildly ahead, for maybe it was too late to accomplish what her cousin Bill did hire her to do. But instead of finding Ian stretch out rigid on the bed, she buck up into him standing cautiously by the dresser, immaculately dressed in a navy blue suit, stretching out his right arm and then his left; before going on to twist his left foot one way and then the other; eyes hopeful yet wary at the same time.

'Lamb of God! Ian, is you this?' She reach out her hands to clasp him tight to her chest, but Ian only fan her one side and continue to flex the muscles in his back one way, before tilting and arching his hips and spine the other way.

Bill brought him a pair of crutches with his name engraved in silver on them, and Ian would vigorously hop round the house unassisted, blind to Miss Dimple's furtive movements behind him, just in case . . . And by the time Dale see Ian the Friday evening, the merriment had danced back into his eyes and a trembling radiance striped his entire person.

The lines that used to cross his forehead only partway, streak all the way across now and the crinkles return to the corner of his left eye. His words became less thick and cloudy as his tongue pick

100

up more and more strength and his jaws regain elasticity. The apartment start to shudder again with the shrill ring of his musical laughter, even though often times it sounded to Dale as if it were near the point of hysteria; almost as if, if Ian didn't grin and laugh out loud at the slightest joke, any moment now, one half of his face would suddenly tighten up again, lose its elasticity and his tongue would fall flat and heavy like cement to the floor of his mouth.

One morning as him make his way down to breakfast, Ian accidentally slip on the polished tile and tumble down the stairs, head first, one step after another. But him didn't even grimace or utter out a shout of pain. When Miss Dimple dash to the scene, hands on her head, satisfaction rigid in her eyes, and reach to help him up, Ian lunge after her with the crutch nearest in reach, almost bouncing out one of her eyes.

'You not as strong as you think,' she bawl out, ducking her head. 'For you won't eat. You meagre down to nothing.'

But the coughing which had ceased throughout the duration of the stroke burst out of his lungs once again drowning out whatever else she was planning to say.

Outside on the verandah one night, while sitting in the dark, Ian ask after Nevin. There were enough lights from the houses across the street to show faces, the occasional gleam of white teeth, the burning brilliance of eyes, Ian's a duller charcoal than Dale's. Glancing at the huddled mass lean over on crutches beside him, Dale wasn't sure what to say, where to start. Him feel as if Ian was gone, that the closeness that use to bind them, did slide down from off them shoulders, and like a cloak that wasn't necessary any longer, did drop noiselessly by them feet. Him wasn't sure where to start.

Two days after the fountain event, Nevin left a fat white parcel at the post office for Dale. Dale bring it home to Loxley's apartment the evening and slip it underneath his desk and didn't turn the white of his eyes to look at it again for three whole days. But during that time, him was like a man possessed. The brilliant white of the parcel haunt him, its sheer bulk weigh on him. For three days him could neither eat nor sleep, and the hair on his face grew in rough and thick. When him finally muster up enough courage to tear the letter open and read it, him stretch out on Loxley's black leather couch in the living room, hold his belly and cow-bawl for several hours, his mouth pressed against the nipples of the velvet cushions.

It was Loxley who had to kneel down on the floor and pick them up the evening. Photographs. About twenty or so. Ripped to shreds. At first Loxley try to match Dale's head to the rest of a torso hugged in a suit or on the beach in shorts, but so many. So many scattered parts. Then there was the ring, the one Dale saved two whole years to buy, with 'Nevin' engraved on the stone, pounded flat with the head of a hammer. Little gold pieces, tie-pins, cuff-links, completely disfigured. There were letters too, from Dale's eight-week stay in Haiti sponsored by the school, his first year. Those Loxley just fold up neat and tie together with a piece of cord after trying without success to match up the dates and paragraphs, to assemble page numbers in order. For two weeks Dale couldn't speak. Lost his voice completely. Could only communicate to Loxley by scribbling notes on scraps of paper.

Dale turn to Ian. How to explain that after five years with Nevin, there wasn't anything to show except deep wounds that embed permanent grooves in his heart. How to explain that even after Nevin hurt him so bad, Dale still wanted to see him, to embrace him, but have to constantly force himself not to go back to the apartment, not to call, his shame was so great. Outside the wind complained, turning over leaves and plastic sweetie wrappers with circular gestures. The place was suddenly cover over with mist, the lighted eyes of houses across the street shining brightly, dotting the night.

'I move out.'

Ian turn on him, dark eyes flashing feverishly. A vein start to vibrate in his forehead, him tap the floor impatiently with the tips of his crutches. 'Move out!'

Dale nod, averting his eyes.

'After all that Nevin give you? After all that him do for you? You turn your back and move out?'

'But Ian, you going on as if I wasn't planning it all along.' Dale's voice was beginning to bristle.

But Ian didn't hear him.

'Nevin give you house. Pay your school fee. Give you trips aboard. Offer you a partnership in his business.' His voice was trembling, becoming more and more hysterical. 'And you throw all that back in his face. You know what I would do to get that? You know how grateful I'd be?'

Then there was quiet. Him wheeze softly. Dale sigh deep and look out into the dark. Yes, him get plenty.

It was starting to rain. Lightning streak across the sky, illuminating the violence in Ian's eyes. 'I suppose you going to say him didn't love you enough. But as far as I can see Dale, it seems as if you wouldn't know love even if it knock you in your face. But you must be happy now, with your own place, your own money, paying you own rent, you own school fee.'

Dale turn and look deep in Ian's face. There wasn't any proudness remaining in his high cheekbones, any sturdiness in the muscles of his jaw. 'Well, I not exactly paying full rent. I living with someone.'

'Another man?'

Dale nod.

'You left Nevin for another man?' The anger was receding out of Ian's eyes, out of his voice.

'Yeah. Him's a lawyer like Bill. Generous, easy-going.'

And at first it was just a chuckle that jerk up from Ian's throat, escaping from between thin lips. But then the laugh grew feverish, irrepressible, even infectious. For Dale himself started to grin, not really certain why, but happy nonetheless that him'd at least quell Ian's jealousy for the time being, restore the friendship back to an even keel, implant the poison back in himself. A spasm of cough followed by several more back to back interrupt the laughter and when that finally ceased, Ian was quiet again. The vein continue to pulse big in his forehead.

'Him treat you OK?'

Dale shrug. 'Agreeable. Sometimes his conversation's as flat as a sidewalk, but him don't really ask for much.'

'Him give you that topaz on you little finger?'

Dale look down on his little finger and nod. From the very beginning Loxley been buying gifts: tie-pins, cuff-links, socks, briefs, fountain pens, colognes. Sometimes Dale would come home to find the bed cover over with little boxes wrap-up in Christmas paper and Loxley grinning like a fox, hands clasp behind him. Then him would demand that Dale try on the silk tie with the linen shirt, that him wear the bath robe around the house and the flimsy briefs to bed. But Dale couldn't find in them the same pleasure that use to stir him when Nevin offer gifts.

For each one of Loxley's gifts wasn't free, each one of them had an invisible string attached, a demand. Him couldn't wear them and walk free. And even though Dale had special feelings for Loxley, for his kindness and generosity and opulence, him still wasn't safe. Him wanted to be able to pay rent even if it was less than half the amount or buy groceries. For at least then him could still preserve some of his integrity.

'You have to stop it.'

'Stop what?' Dale ask curiously, still fondling the ring.

'This life. This business.' Ian spread his fingers, eyes wavering.

'Why?'

'Cause. You have to.' Him was studying his fingers with much intent now. 'Have to stop it. Have to.'

But Ian was no longer speaking to Dale. Him was carrying on a monologue with himself. Finally Ian spring up off the bench, the heels of his crutches knocking the concrete with a severe crash. 'It have to stop.' Him was shouting now, his face contorted, his body wound up like a top. 'It have to stop.' Him bounce his way up the stairs, Dale following swiftly behind, aghast.

'Ian, what's happening? What have to stop?'

At the top of the darkened stairs, Dale grip Ian by the wrist, but with renewed strength, Ian shrug him off fiercely, bolt inside his room and slam the door behind him, rattling the mirror on the dresser, sending streams of vibration throughout the house.

'Ian?' Dale pound on the door with his fist. 'Ian?' Him wring the door-knob several times, cursing furiously, sweat from his brow sliding into his eyes, blinding him.

But Ian only turn up the volume on the tape player by his bedside and filled the house with Miss Dimple's gospel music, drowning out Dale's commotion outside the door.

Dale turn away. He didn't know what to do anymore. Ian was

104

giving up, losing himself to this unknown disease that had grown roots and was now flourishing rapidly, eating away at Ian little-little, destroying him.

Miss Dimple was waiting at the bottom of the stairs, arms folded satisfactorily across her bosom, victory swimming below the surface of her eyes, trembling on her lips.

'You put him up to this,' Dale roared, hating her all of a sudden. 'You the one causing him to hate himself. To loathe his life. I didn't trust you from the beginning.' Dale march towards her. 'Now I know why. Your religion not about love, it's about hate. You preach hatred and fear.'

Miss Dimple didn't say anything, she waited till Dale was calm then focus her glance at his feet, her voice simmering with humility before starting. 'Please don't blame me, Mr Singleton, for I am not the cause. Ian been going on like this for the past week and a half, now. Sometimes in the middle of the night, when the house quiet-quiet, all the neighbours asleep, him suddenly wake up and start to scream this business bout "it have to stop". Sometimes him fling things round the room, break them up. Sometimes him gather a whole host of newspaper and magazines him keep in a box under his bed and set fire to them. So please don't lay the blame on me, sir.' Then she pause, making sure everything was quiet. 'Yesterday him ask me if him can accompany me to church next Sunday, maybe even set up an appointment for his baptism . . .'

'Ian?' Dale interrupt her, not quite believing. 'Ian want religion?'

'Self same,' she answer meekly, before continuing on victoriously. 'Him even ask me for a Bible. Say him don't own one.'

Dale didn't say anything else. Him just turn away from her and walk slowly out the door, never even bothering to say goodnight, or to pull the door shut behind him, to keep out the strong wind. For why Ian couldn't ask him, Dale? Dale who'd been leading Sunday School for six straight years. Dale who'd been saved since him was sixteen by Pastor Booker. Dale who'd been leading little children into the fold for the past ten years. Dale who'd been administering christenings and baptisms. Now all of a sudden Miss Dimple's religion better than his.

Dale start to walk briskly, his anger mounting, eyes blind to the people standing up on the sidewalk waiting for the bus, to the ones walking fast behind him, ahead. But him was going to show the whole lot, stock and barrel of them that what them think don't count. That him wasn't going to lose faith because of them. Then him remember the conversation with Bill and his steps slowed. Them did meet for a drink as planned, down at New Kingston Hotel, in an umbrellaed seat, overlooking the pool. It was a month ago, the place was flooded with English-accented-tourists tittering gaily, obnoxiously dressed in cut-off jeans and leather sandals. Waitresses dash back and forth crazily in the heat.

Dale did plan to ask Bill for a loan, but each time him open his mouth to utter the request, Bill cut him off with some new observation, some new idea, his eyes grinning, flirtatious. Then all at once Bill's narrow red face sobered, and him ask Dale: 'You praying for Ian?'

'Every day.' Dale's tone was just as sombre.

'Well, him need more than that.' Bill dip his fingers in his drink and swirl the ice-cubes around and around thoughtfully. 'Him need to give up this nonsense, this man-loving shit. You too.' Him refuse to meet Dale's hardened gaze, and steady his eyes instead on the coffee liquor in his glass. 'God punishing him, making him poorly. It's happening all over, abroad, everywhere. So this physical therapy business every other day not going to help, take it from me.'

Dale pick up his newspaper from off the metal table and push back his chair. Now him realise why him didn't trust Bill. Now him know why him didn't like his oily grin. His sweet mouth. His kiss-me-ass kindness.

'No. Please don't leave!' Bill's voice was hoarse, him grab Dale's wrist.

People were beginning to stare at them. Dale didn't care. Him shrug off Bill's hand, soft and sweaty on his wrist.

'What about you?' Dale grind out at him, his temper mounting, forgetting about the loan. 'What you do with your man-loving shit? Your nonsense? Every Saturday night you latch your backside on a stool at Clovy's and watch every man that walk by from out the corner of your eye.'

'I go for the music, the crowd, but I gave it up.' His voice was low, trembling, as if him wanting to cry. 'Two years ago.'

Dale had left then, had blanked out the entire conversation from his mind. But now as him walk slowly along, it return to pinch him, jab at his sides like spurs. Ten years ago when him accepted Christ as his Personal Saviour, his Holy Redeemer, him did ask God to accept him too, with all his faults, all his failures. Him did make a covenant between himself and God. But now the devil was rearing its ugly head in the shape of Ian's illness, in the form of Miss Dimple's religion, in the image of Bill; it was testing his faith, demanding that Dale choose, choose between Salvation and the love between men.

There wasn't a light in Nevin's apartment, it seemed desolate and dead next to Mrs Morgan's house that was alive and bursting with tension. The huddled masses crouch over on her verandah turned out to be cardboard boxes scattered across the tile, tie-up with English cord, others wrap around with masking tape. Mr Morgan was cranking up the chair, wheezing loudly. Dale walk past him, nodding howdy-do, and on to the verandah. Mrs Morgan appear in the doorway, breathing loud, a big heavy box in her hands. She dump it off at Dale's feet.

'She going to marry him.' Her voice dragged with emotion.

Dale didn't dare say a word. Him was caught dead in the middle of a fight between Mrs Morgan and Rose.

'Can you believe it, Dale?' Her arms were akimbo, her bosom heaving with emotion. 'Make up invitations behind my back, send them out. At the last minute she tell me. But that don't even bother me so much like the fact that she going to marry this nasty-headed, no good Rastafarian thief.'

'His head cleaner than mine and yours put together,' Rose pipe out from somewhere close. Dale turn towards the sound of her voice. 'And him not a thief.'

'Walk off and don't back answer me, gal,' Mrs Morgan shout out, swinging around towards the voice. 'You don't have ambition.

107

Just like your daddy's side of family.' On the carport, Mr Morgan wheezed even louder. 'After all the schooling I put you through, this is the gratitude. You going to marry this shit-house, this natty dread man, who have his red ganja eyes on my money.'

'His eyes clearer than mine and yours put together.' The voice pipe out again.

'You hear how she love to give lip?' Mrs Morgan swing back to Dale. 'You hear her? Is my hand she want to feel across her jaw, you know. Is my heavy foot she want to feel stepping up and down in her stomach, you know.'

'Heh, heh,' Rose laugh out loud. 'That is going to be the day.'

Mrs Morgan's stout frame stiffen, then set off towards the voice, feet dragging underneath her.

Dale wanted to leave. This wasn't why him come. This wasn't what him wanted to hear. Then there was a loud crash. Followed by a grunt. Dale close his eyes and waited. Stop his breath and listened. The wheelchair ceased its creaking. Then Mrs Morgan was out again, dragging another box behind her.

'She have to go, Dale. She have to go.' Mrs Morgan shake her head. 'Can you imagine, a Rastaman?' Disbelief stain her voice. 'I ask her worthless brother to speak to her. But him only make promises, with his lying mouth. "Yes, Yes, I will talk to her." But up till now, Dale. Up till now, nothing.'

Dale smile. That was Nevin, all right. Him would never tell his mother, no, but him wasn't going to do what she ask, either. Him would always listen to her attentive, but never hear.

Then Mrs Morgan take hold of Dale's hand. 'Maybe you can talk to her, Dale.'

Dale stiffen, turning away from her gaze, the sorrow in her eyes.

'Maybe you can show her right from wrong, advise her. I can't have a Rastaman in the family, Dale. Anything but a Rastaman. You see that boy's hair? You see his eyes? Dale. I can smell him anywhere, him so stink of that ganja. Can you imagine me grandchildren, Dale? All of them with this Rasta head. This Hail, Selassi, shit. This natty dread head tie up with a nasty rag. Then run come call me, granny. I would rather die.' She was starting to cry, her fingers gripping on to Dale's tightly.

Dale hope Nevin wouldn't show up all of a sudden. The last

108

thing him wanted was for Mrs Morgan to drag him into this ugliness with her daughter.

Then she lean forward, her eyes glowing wickedly and whisper to Dale: 'Thank God for all the miscarriages.'

And Dale knew then that it was she who'd secretly induced them. Three miscarriages in all. Him wanted to leave now. But the grip on his hand was tight. 'Mrs Morgan,' his voice was timid, the crab trembling, 'I was just passing. I just wanted to stop and say hello. I really don't want to get involved.'

She drop Dale's hand suddenly and pull in her breath, taking in her stomach as well. 'Even you turn against me.' Her voice was cutting. 'Even you turn against me.' Her eyes were cold and hard, her voice rising.

Dale look down at his shoes. Cars driving pass slowed down. Drivers turn heads to look at the bright lights on the verandah and at the boxes, listen to the commotion. Dale wonder which would be Nevin's.

'Look, Mrs Morgan,' his voice was stern. 'I want to help.' Him wanted to run too. She kill all of Rose's children. Three in all. What wouldn't she do? And Rose was her own daughter, even. Her own flesh and blood. 'I really want to help,' his eyes watery, raise up to meet hers, but only cold and rigid cement blocks return the gaze. 'But, Rose is a big woman. She thirteen years older than me. I can't tell her how to run her life, how to . . .'

'Even you. Even you take the side of the Rastaman. I leave you to Nevin.' Her voice was solemn, mocking.

'What you mean you leave me to Nevin?' Dale was agitated now, the crab trembling. 'What you mean?' But then him stop. Rose was starting to laugh in the background, Mr Morgan's wheezing had subsided. It was him and Mrs Morgan now. Dale spin around and danced his way through the maze of boxes. 'Look, Mrs Morgan,' him call out over his shoulders, from out the gate. 'I have to go. I really have to go.' And him was gone.

Dale wander along aimlessly. The moon was shining. The rain had stopped. Him could see the roads clearly, make out faces, the shape of noses, him walk by the well-lit cottages lining the street, ignoring dogs that yap cautiously from behind sculptured hedges. What she mean by she was leaving me up to Nevin, anyway? What did she mean, exactly? Mrs Morgan, the very same woman who gave him the speech that night about good and evil wasn't any blasted better than Miss Kaysen. Both of them don't like people different from themselves. Oh God! Dale spit sudden.

For there wasn't anybody down at the church more sanctimonious than Mrs Morgan. Those Sundays she attend, she was usually the first to give testimony – to acknowledge how God has changed her life. Her prayers were always longer, her wails louder. Those Sundays she attend, she was usually the first to stretch a bony finger and point, to cast the first stone. Yet, back at home, she had crippled her husband, killed all her grandchildren, and every member of the congregation had squeezed them eyes shut for fear of being blinded by her wickedness. Now here was Dale, no better than any of them. For the opportunity had risen, had presented itself right under his nose, here was the chance for him to point out right from wrong, but instead him was turning and running away.

Him could just see it now, plain as day, the moment him should ever take careless and challenge Mrs Morgan. First him would take a deep breath, tuck in his stomach, pulling up himself to his full 67 inches. And in the gentlest voice possible, tell her, 'But Mrs Morgan, what about Rose's happiness? You married and have your children, why not give her a chance? The man come, for five years him been coming, no doubt him mean well.' And then him would make the mistake of saying to her, 'It's not right what you doing, Mrs Morgan, it's not right atall.'

Briskly, she would wave him to a halt with a quick swing of her wrist. 'You want to talk about right from wrong, Dale Singleton? You want to talk about it?' Then she would pause to laugh loud and long, nostrils quivering wide, her false teeth glimmering. But then she would stop just as sudden as she began, and her eyes would be stone, cold. 'Suppose I was to tell them down at the church about the nasty life you lead over there?' and she would toss her head careless in the direction of Nevin's apartment, 'Suppose I was to tell them about the sin and shame you living in, the worst form of sin, ever . . .?'

110

And at this point, Dale would stop listening to her, for him could see now the entire congregation gathered around for his excommunication. Deacon Roache, own self, would carry it out, his short fat neck slumped into the collar of his white shirt. And instead of speaking from the pulpit, him would make his way down to the front pew, so people could see the emotions clearly imprinted in his eyes, red from sipping too much wine. 'Brothers and sisters,' him would start off tentatively, pausing to gulp or to squeeze back the eye water trembling in the corners of his eyes (him would want to maximise on everybody's emotions).

Then him would sigh deep and start off again, his voice a few octaves higher, tone a little bit sturdier. 'Brothers and sisters.' Again him would pause to make certain him grab everyone's attention, even those in the back likely to be nodding off in the heat. 'The Devil is among us.' And the women in the front row would shriek out amens, wave handkerchiefs, fan hands, handbags, Bibles. 'Yes, my people, a wolf is among us in sheep's clothing.'

Him would start to walk slowly down the aisle, his black shoes noiseless on the rug, fondling his tie with each step, head bent as if in deep sorrow, his barrel-figure barely contained in the grey suit. 'We were fooled for some time, brothers and sisters, but as the Book of Revelations tells us, we shall not be fooled for long. By the mark on his back we shall know him.' Pause to accommodate more shrieks. More wails. 'The beast is among us. And he is very sly, brothers and sisters, very sly. Like Judas who betrayed Christ, he has eaten among us, worshipped with us, to him we've entrusted our deepest and most intimate concerns, to him we've entrusted our children . . .' More shrieks and amens and flagging of handkerchiefs. 'Only to have him betray us.'

Then him would stop finally at Dale's pew. And everyone in the row would twitch nervously from fear. But Deacon Roache's eyes would first pass over John Brown who committed adultery with one of the girls in the choir last year, and his eyes would pass over Eric Tom who beat his wife constantly, Elma Tubs who was excommunicated from Ebenezer Open Bible for stealing church

111

money and many others, before finally coming to rest on Dale. No other sin was as great as Dale's . . .

A tall thin holy-looking man in a white robe was handing out leaflets and preaching in a loud voice under the white glare of the street lamp, further up the street. Several women were gathered around, some crying, others singing hymns. Dale didn't know what to do, suddenly him felt trapped. To his right was the sign leading to Nanny Sharp's. Maybe him should go in, him didn't want to have to walk pass the preacher or the men squatting down at the bus stop, faces lost in shadows, conversations muted, the fiery tips of cigarettes glowing then dulling, smoke swirling out into the darkness. His shadow amble on ahead nervously, to the right, all the caution heaped on to Ian thrown to the wind. Him walk soundless, footsteps lost on the concrete, now grass. The moon had slipped under. Dale melted into the dark. Trees resemble men with hard bodies, eagerly waiting. Dale pounce on, uncertain where him was going exactly, slowing down now and again to look around him, to listen for sounds. Him had to leave the church. It was impossible to continue on like this. His days heaped in hypocrisy. In lies. Suddenly a heavy hand grip his shoulder. Him stiffen, heart galloping in his chest.

'Easy.' The voice was gentle, almost tender. 'Isn't this why you came?'

Dale didn't answer. All of a sudden, his voice failed him. Not to the fear of whether this man would kill him, would beat him up and rob him of the thirty dollars in his wallet, but to the embarrassment, the shame. For now him wasn't any better than Ian or Bill or countless others who come. The hand carefully guided Dale towards the overhanging branches of a tree, side stepping tree stumps, puddles of water.

And like a cape that was protecting him, all the embarrassment suddenly dropped to Dale's feet and him could catch all the nuances of the perfume that clung to the man's body, the bitter, acrid odour of car grease that settle permanently under his nails, in his pores, the bitter sweet smell of perspiration under his arms, on his neck, especially putrid in the heat. All awaken Dale's

112

hunger. The coarse jeans, the cold buckle, the hard body rub vigorously against Dale. The man was taller, his shirt was open at the throat, wiry hairs graze Dale's neck. The hand, downy with hair, move across Dale's chin and started to open the buttons at the collar of his shirt. It clamp around one of Dale's breast. It was hard, calloused, rough, fingers: short, thick. The fingers moulded and squeezed and tugged.

Against him Dale lay, almost swooning, the heat licking away at his ears, his chiselled cheeks, his massive throat, the turmoil coursing through his veins. And all of a sudden, Dale didn't care about anything. Not about God or Deacon Roache, Ian's disease or Bill's hypocrisy or Miss Kaysen's craziness. Him didn't care about Nevin, about Loxley, about Mrs Morgan and Rose's pending marriage. All him wanted was this man, this burly brute with the callous hands and acrid breath, growing heavier and warmer against Dale's neck, this Don Juan with the soft effete voice and pungent perfume.

Then Dale wanted to turn to see who this man was, to put his mouth on the man's lips, to trace the grooves on the face with his fingers, to peer into the darkness of his eyes, but the man's grip was like iron, his thighs ribbed against Dale's legs like steel. Him start to suck Dale's throat, cracked lips making clucking sounds, stubbles on his chin sharply digging into Dale's neck, while one hand slip down to liberate flesh barely contained behind the tissue-like membrane of Dale's trousers. Dale brace forward into the cupped hand, then backward against the man. The short, stubby fingers were tugging with the buttons to his silk trousers. But the fingers, now sweaty, slap violently at Dale's. Dale quickly retrieve them out of harm's way.

With a slight rustle, like a dog shaking off cold water, the trousers drop to Dale's ankles, gathering like the edges of a dancer's taffeta gown over his patent leather shoes. And Dale savour every contraction, every expansion, every twinge of muscle, every palpitation in every corner as the man's fingers encircle, fondle, run deftly up and down, returning again and again, sometimes using only two fingers, sometimes the whole calloused hand. Then the hand was suddenly gone from Dale's raw and blistered nipple and the clinking of a buckle and the tinkle of the

113

zip rip the night with such violence, all of a sudden Dale open his eyes to the lights and sounds of traffic on the main road several yards from the tips of his patent leather shoes.

Him breathe in the air charged with flower smells, rotting wood, damp dirt. People pass quickly back and forth on the narrow dirt road close-by, low conversations and spiralling laughter ringing loud into the night. But them could see neither Dale nor the stranger, for the large limbs of the willow trees served as chameleons in the dark.

Hands grip his hips, forcing him forward. Dale stumble, the coins from his pocket and keys sing out, the effete voice released a curse, but the hands, vice-like, steadied him, and with much swiftness and dexterity, as if well familiar with the narrow route, the man rip open soft folds pushing his way into flesh, pummelling and churning and crushing until the sound easing from his throat was like that of a hog whimpering quietly in pain. Then him was gone. And Dale was alone. Flooded with guilt. With shame. With pleasure. Him stoop down to pull up his trousers, all the while looking around, behind him, in front, to the side. Him squint his eyes, stop his breath so as to hear better any faint sounds, but the footsteps retreating on the grass were just as noiseless as them'd appeared.

Loxley was waiting up on the leather couch out in the living room when Dale turn the lock and push open the door. It was late. The room in complete darkness except for the lighted hands of the clock on the wall. The room silent except for Loxley's rattling and wheezing chest.

'You all right?' Him leap off the couch and rush towards Dale, concern thick in his voice.

'Of course!' Dale ease out of his way, suddenly annoyed. Then embarrassed. Then ashamed.

'You didn't call or anything. It's running into three now. I thought maybe something . . .'

'No. No. I was at Ian's.' Dale's voice soften. His eyes shift restlessly around the room, unable to face Loxley, to hurt him with guilty eyes. The salty fresh scent of sea shells oozed from his pores. Him was sure Loxley could smell it. The air was so thick, so cloudy with it. 'The illness, you know. Him was just crying and crying. So, I just stayed.' Dale shake his head and sighed. 'But you right, I really should've called. Sorry. I just lost track of time.'

Loxley walk back towards the couch and pick up the cigarette he'd been smoking from off the coffee table. Him inhale, scratch his head. The robe hang loose around him, exposing thin legs. Him exhale, replace the cigarette, then started walking towards Dale again, grinning this time, the alarm gone from his face. 'Well, I just glad you OK.' Him pause. 'Can I have a hug?'

Suddenly Dale didn't like his teeth. The canines were too long, the tips jagged.

'Oh God, Loxley. Just let me shower first.' Him know one thing would lead to another, then Loxley would see traces of the stranger on his legs.

'Why?' Suddenly the grin was gone.

Dale breathed heavily, backing off. 'I just feel sweaty and dirty. I walked all the way from Ian's house. I just wanted to think, to breathe in some fresh air. Shake the depression.'

'Is Nevin again, isn't it?' Loxley's voice was hard, eyes cold. Him walk back to the couch, tighten the belt around his waist, shutting the door to his robe.

Dale didn't say anything. Him look hard at Loxley's sagging shoulders and flat behind and sigh deep, wishing all of a sudden that him could love Loxley. Loxley who was so good to him. Would give him the world. 'Listen,' his voice was tired. Loxley was taking quick puffs off his cigarette, Adam's apple bobbing nervously. Him stare ahead, looking at nothing in particular, slanted eyes hooded. 'Listen,' Dale started again, 'in two-twos I'll be out.' Him try to sound jovial. 'OK?'

Loxley didn't answer.

Inside the shower, the lukewarm water beat steady down Dale's back, washing away all traces of the stranger, his firm grip, coarse hammer hands, the sea-shell scent. Dale wasn't sure how long him stayed in the shower. But when him walk out, with the white towel wrapped tight around his waist, shoulders and back still bespeckled with water, Loxley was stretch-out fast asleep on the couch, mouth ajar, cigarette burning steady in the tray. Dale lean over and watched him for a while, the stolid rise and fall of his chest, the slight snores that escape now and again. The physical resemblances to Nevin weren't there anymore, his own features had set in and with it a fierce jealousy. Dale stub the cigarette, turn off the lamp, heave Loxley on to his shoulder and tuck him into bed. Then Dale kiss him tenderly on the lips, drinking in the stench of gin on Loxley's breath. Him had to find somewhere else to go. Didn't like the pain that was constantly dancing below the surfaces of Loxley's narrow brown eyes. Didn't like how it made him feel.

Dale didn't get an invitation to the baptism, but the Sunday morning him get up early nonetheless, dressed himself in a spanking navy suit with wide lapels and black striped tie, board the number 43 bus and make his way slowly up the dirt path leading to the narrow little church with high steeples perched on top the hill. When Dale noiselessly step inside the church with its heavy red rug padding the floor, and stained glass windows of glossy-eyed madonnas looking wistfully outside at the cemetery fenced around with barb wire, the barrel-faced minister was already bowed at the altar, leading the congregation in prayers.

Dale spot Miss Dimple's black felt hat trimmed with ripe apples and pears right away, in a row of other hats just as colourfully displayed, Bill's snow-white hair and expensive business suit and the people to be baptised sprinkling the gaily dressed congregation with white robes. A peal of coughing sing out into the quiet droning of the minister indicating Ian's whereabouts at once. Dale take a seat next to a lady, heavily perfumed with talcum powder, wearing a flaming red hat bedecked with white hibiscus whose pink stamens shot out into the air.

Soon the prayer was over and the minister beckoned to the baptism members to make them way up to the altar. Slowly the angels in white rise from off them seats and sounds of 'please excuse me', 'sorry' and 'thanks' pervade the room as them make way clumsily out each pew and down the narrow aisle. The organist organise the wings of her spectacles around her wide ears, run her tongue swiftly over her parted lips before deftly running her bony fingers up and down the beige and black keyboard, discharging vivacious melody throughout the church.

Outside the window, Dale watch young fellows sweep up nails, pieces of broken bottles, dead leaves from the dirt path leading to the cistern where Ian was to be baptised. A very tall woman was standing at the edge of the cistern, skilfully guiding a net over the green surface of the water, as she skim out dead mosquitoes and worms, the taut muscles of her arm rising tremendously against the thin cotton material of her white frock. Up front the young angels of God were assembled. Dale spot Ian immediately from the sea of faces. Liver marks discolour his cheeks and forehead and his neck was slumped in the collar of his white robe.

The doctor did say the stroke would come back when Ian least expect it. Maybe while rising after bending down to tie his shoelace; or one night while lying in bed, flat on his back, feet fold at the ankles, rolling back and forth some thought or other; it might be in the middle of a laugh with his mouth wide-open, teeth on display, eyes wet with joy, hands outstretched and trembling with merriment. Then the stroke would strike, stiffening every joint, every limb, every corpuscle in his body.

'But what about medication?' Dale did ask the doctor, refusing to be undaunted. They'd met out in the waiting room, one afternoon Dale did accompany Ian to physical therapy.

'Well . . .' The doctor sigh long, inspecting the soiled tips of his white Bata shoes, then the rounded mouth of Dale's black loafers, all the while rocking his squat little body back and forth, hands clasp behind him. 'Maybe if you get him to a hospital abroad, maybe them can help him there. But . . .' Him pause again to shake his head, eyes dead on the floor, 'out here, all I can think about is that fellow, Brookes, the one that slip into the coma . . .'

On the way home, Dale ask Ian if him want to stop in at the bar. It was about seven the evening, dusk just beginning to shadow the sky, a fiery orange, a pale purple, to spread chills. At first Ian hesitate, eyes dropping at once to the curved handle of the cane shivering in his hand, to the excess material of his trousers billowing out around his shrunken hips and legs. But just as quickly, his eyes light up and his pace quicken. Dale wonder with suppressed panic if Nevin was going to be there and with whom. Just last week, a note arrive from the registrar's office at his school claiming that the tuition for that quarter was paid. But Dale didn't want to have anything to do with Nevin, not now, not next week, not ever. The wound was still wide open, raw. Him call the registrar's office at once and tell them it was a mistake, that him was on medical leave for a semester, that them should return the cheque to sender.

It was early, but already the smell of salt and leather and sweat and stale beer and sounds of loud music and edges of conversations grip the air. Nevin wasn't anywhere in sight. Ian wanted to dance right away, and after the first tune ended and Dale noticed how the sweat soaked Ian's underarms and back, wash his face, him suggest right away that them should stop. But Ian still wanted to swing his arms – dark eyes burning without any brilliance; to gyrate his hips – head fling back, mouth slightly ajar; to draw attention to his slender self, like when Dale had seen him first with Nevin.

And then the coughing started and at first Ian shrug it off, grinning even wider, the burning brilliance of his eyes gleaming more and more dull, but then him couldn't keep in the cough anymore and it burst out of him, causing the sharp edges of conversation to hiss to a dull drone, then silence, and eyes that weren't turned on him before suddenly to widen, jaws to drop low. Slowly Dale lead him off the dance floor, and the crowd created a passageway and him lead the cough-racked Ian past the bar, and the jukebox to a quiet spot near the door. A fellow and his boyfriend offer up stools. Another arrive with a roll of toilet paper, somebody else with a glass of water. And with the onslaught of cool and fresh air, the cough subsided to only a grunt escaping Ian's lips now and again.

'You want to go?' Dale ask, after the vigour had returned to Ian's jaws, conversations had picked up again, heads had turned away from them. But no amount of jostling would get Ian to budge. Him just sit down, back curved forward, hands hung still over his knees, and his eyes, calm and grave inside narrow sockets, were starting to glance inwards. Dale knew then that nothing was going to move Ian.

The entire ceremony lasted ninety minutes. There were nine people to be baptised. Ian was number seven. The congregation file singly between the minister's flowing black robe, trimmed with red and purple lace around the collar and down the front, curving generously over his wide belly, as him march his way slowly, head bowed in prayer, over to the cistern. Dale was standing at the way back of the line, partly hidden among shrubbery, people him didn't know. All around him women were crying out loud amens, faces glistening with tears. Dale spot Miss Dimple's hat and slide out of her view, him spot Andrea and a fellow with Ian's length and similar bone structure to the face, then him spot Bill approaching, hazel eyes gleaming, face slightly sallow from the overbearing humidity.

Dale take the hand, though not really wanting to. For now Ian would turn out like Bill and this wasn't what religion should be used for, to hide behind like a veil, to plunge into like a dream. Him should be able to accept himself and his religion, embrace the two like a twin. Not suppress one, while the other reign triumphant.

'Yes, it's a pleasant ceremony.' Dale's voice was dead-pan. 'But what's next if Ian doesn't get well? Who you going to bargain with then? The devil?'

'Dale, you can see for yourself. Ian's not getting any better . . . Dale?'

Quickly him sidestep Bill and wander on toward the crowd gathered around the cistern. Him peer in from underneath somebody's arms. The chubby black hands of the minister were cradling the head of a young girl. Fat lips open and closed, voice rumbled on and on, tones soothing. Before him the girl's eyes were squeezed shut, her thin face cringed, her slight frame shake violently inside the gown. All around him women shriek out as if in pain, as the minister dunk one, then another, the water splashing occasionally up on to his chest, wetting his face, his white pointed shoes. Several times him pause to drink from a tumbler somebody hand him, to mop his temples and the folds of his chin with a spotless white handkerchief appearing suddenly from out of the crowd as the midday heat raged tremendously and the sun beat down mercilessly from above. Blotches appeared at the armpits of the robe staining it a pale yellow, patches of cloth suck to his broad back.

Then it was Ian's turn. And a thin wail started out from somewhere close to Dale, rising above the dull drone of the minister, sending a quiet hush over the piercing shrieks. One moment the wail was right behind Dale, next moment it was gone, dancing in and out of the crowd, pausing behind the wide concrete columns of the church, now skipping over sharp-edged rocks, echoing against the walls of the cistern. Dale didn't see her, the woman, tall and erect like a pine tree, busily sifting through the crowd, her face tight with emotions as the wails rip themselves from the edges of her belly and slap violently against the rippled surface of the water.

Election day dawned on a very grey and somewhat chilly Thursday morning. But that didn't stop the turnout. Long lines spill out of polling stations and into the streets, slowing down traffic as people enter to dip thumbs in red ink, then press hard next to the X before going on to work. The days leading up election had been relatively peaceful. Fifteen dead, fifty injured. Only three buildings bombed. Last time them did set fire to Port Royal's police station, killing one third of the officers stationed there. Dale did have to beg Loxley to register. Say him had no interest, for it was the same two evils running every time. This annoyed Dale for these were exactly his thoughts before meeting Nevin. 'At least you have the opportunity to vote.' His tone erupted much harder than he'd expect, echoing Nevin. 'Some places you can't vote atall.' Dale did try to soften his voice. But not even that could erase the shadows that constantly danced across Loxley's face ever since the day him came home and found the apartment section of the newspaper Dale had carelessly left open wide on the kitchen counter, several listings encircled in black.

'What is this, Dale?' His hands stretch out towards the counter.

Dale didn't quite know what to say. How to tell Loxley that him was feeling more and more like a hypocrite each day him stay at the house and pretend him was in love. Him wasn't going to school anymore and since him couldn't bear the long stretches of

120

daylight with Loxley, he'd taken a full-time job at the post office offering to work the night shift. Each morning after Loxley left for work, Dale would sit down and compose a few poems and after him grow bored with that, would clip articles from newspaper and paste them into his scrap book and when that didn't interest him anymore, would dust and tidy the house before taking the bus downtown to browse through store windows, visit Ian, then continue on to work.

At Ian's house, him would hear only the sounds of gospel music piping out of the tape player in his room, for Ian had stopped speaking these days, and Miss Dimple was always preoccupied with dusting and reading the Bible. Dale cut down the amount of time spent at the church. Now him only show up to lead Young People's meeting since it was always easier to lose himself in other people's problems than deal with his own and to teach one section of Sunday School. Him didn't stay for the midday service anymore, or for Bible study. Every time him spot Mrs Morgan approaching, him dodge from her. After work him would frequent the park, eagerly awaiting the moment when the hand would press against his shoulder; each bringing its own peculiar brand of perfume: the clorox bleach on a white shirt; armpits and chest reeking of Brut; or the coconut-flavoured hair oil. Sometimes him would reach out his hand to feel for grooves alongside the corners of a mouth, his heart hammering loudly . . .

But here was Loxley looking at him, eyes getting watery, lips beginning to waver. And Dale resented nothing more than to feel cornered, boxed in. 'Loxley, you don't expect me to stay here forever? This is your place. Surely you must want your privacy back?'

But with that, only tears would follow, for with Loxley, his tone was always the same grave hardness. And since it would hurt Dale every time Loxley start to cry, for it would always make him feel guilty, him would just grab his sweater and leave the house.

One night while walking towards the bus stop, a silver Austin Cambridge pull up alongside Dale. At first him thought it was Alexander, for it resembled the car his wife used to drive. It was a little after midnight. The road was dark, and the wind, blowing a little more briskly than usual, fling back muted sounds from the howls of his co-workers up ahead. Dale did tell them to go on, him would catch up, just have to run back and pick up his sweater. But as Dale stepped closer and peered in, anxious to see his friend again, it wasn't Alexander atall, but Nevin who stared back at him. Dale pull in his stomach and started to walk fast, away from the car, chest heaving. Him wondered what Nevin wanted now. Business must be going well. Him buy a new car.

The car was slowly following Dale, the person shout out his name. It echoed in the darkness. But Dale walk on hurriedly, him didn't have anything to say to Nevin. Not to someone who would destroy those letters. It was ten months into the relationship when Dale wrote them. The first time they'd been apart. Every day Dale wrote, telling about Haiti, how so many of the customs similar, yet different, especially those peculiar to the French. But mainly Dale would write to say him missed lying in bed till late (especially on Sundays when Nevin didn't have to join his mother in the market), talking, crying, laughing, making love, telling stories, feeling embarrassed, sad, frustrated. Nevin had made it so easy for Dale to trust, and like a fool he'd plunged in blindly, now and again coming up anxious, eyes wild, wondering if Nevin would fall out of love, would find someone else. But Nevin was always there, reassuring, admiring, and Dale would feel safe again, drunk with love.

'Dale.'

Dale continue on. Behind him the clatter was loud, uneven. All that was gone now. Nevin allow Johnney to come in and destroy it.

'Dale.'

Slowly Dale turned around. 'Nevin look . . .' The hardness dropped from his voice. 'What happen to your hand?' Nevin's left hand was wrapped in a cast. Him shift it slightly. But without waiting for an answer, Dale continued on. 'Look, I have nothing to say to you. What you want from me?'

Up close, Nevin look thinner, face slightly bruised. Jaws jut out more. Eyes without sheen. 'Dale, let's just talk. The packet. Oh

122

God.' Him sigh long and look up the road to the darkness. 'I lost my head. I lost . . .'

'The bus will be here any minute now. So speak quick. What you want?'

Clumsily Nevin reach over, probably to embrace Dale, both arms were outstretched, the one with the cast not as high.

'What the fuck you want?' Dale had sprung back. As if anticipating the move. Up ahead, the talking had become louder, more agitated. Somebody call out that the bus was coming. Dale heard the rumbling of the engine. Then the glare from the headlamps fill the dark. And without even saying goodbye, Dale sprinted off in the direction of the bus, his body, now elongated and silhouetted silver against the light.

November 1978

The two were running barefoot through the tall guinea grass, Dale with paper bag for his godmother clutch tight to his shirtless chest, Nevin, ahead, wearing short trousers, shouting against wind that was picking up sounds, throwing them back. Pass the coop stink with chicken shit, the latrine, rabbit pen, pass the apple tree with rotting fruit underneath, Dale race, little feet dodging sharp-edged stones, dancing over piles of cow shit, pieces of wood, dead tree stumps. Already Nevin was at the stone wall, thin arms flailing, getting ready to climb over into the cow pen where Dale's father's cows lay chewing. Them flick off flies with bushy tails, turning large curious eyes to watch the two little boys in short khaki trousers.

Then Dale didn't see Nevin anymore. Him see instead the bull, red eyes gleaming, stamping towards him, snorting. Dale stop, chest heaving, breath loud in his ears. The earth around him trembled with the steady gallop of the bull. The orange trees seem to pull back, huddle together, same way the potato slips growing between each tree, the yam hills with stick rooted to help vines grow.

Dale start to back-back, his heels treading careful through tall grass, over stones, the bag from his mother with the pudding crushed on his heart. Thump, thump, the earth around him shake. And still no sight of Nevin against the wall, just the mass of black charging, neck bent forward, horns glistening, eyes fiery, unseeing. And the scent of the animal was in Dale's mouth, in his ears. And him couldn't breathe anymore. Everything just feel jammed in the middle of his chest, choking him, blocking off his air.

Dale open his eyes wide. Him open his mouth wide, and only his tongue showed. Him press against his belly for the scream to shoot out, but only air followed and him press again, this time harder, for the bull was upon him and his heels weren't going back anymore, but a ringing came out, a shrill sound like a bell, school bell, no church bell . . .

Dale leap out of the fold-out bed near the door and make his way groggy towards the telephone perched on a table with thin legs near the couch in the living room. It chimed again, jarring the steady rhythms of Loxley's snores from the bedroom. Goose bumps gather themselves on the back of Dale's arms and march down his sides towards the back of his calves. 'Hello.' The receiver was cold against his ears. Then all of a sudden, the machine spring out of Dale's hands and fling itself on the hard tile with a furious clatter. Loxley's snores paused. Then start up again. The lighted hands of the clock on the wall showed twelve minutes past three.

'Hello?'

'Yes, this is Dale.'

'Yes, this is Dale. Who is . . .' Him was starting to wake up. The voice screeched at him.

'Andrea?' Oh God. Dale feel his breathing race in his chest. Ian. Something happen to Ian. The stroke. No coma.

'Say what?'

'You think him dead?'

'Who you talking to, Dale?' It was Loxley. Him switch on the lamp by the telephone. Light flooded the room blinding Dale.

Dale wave away Loxley, his hand chopping the air. 'Andrea?' His voice was desperate. 'Andrea? Listen to me. Andrea, listen.'

'Who is it, Dale?'

'Ian's sister. Something happen to . . .'

'Andrea. Just because him stiff don't mean him dead?'

'OK. I coming now.'

'Rightaway.'

Dale put down the phone. All of a sudden him feel weak, tired, for him'd not too long come in from Ian's birthday party Bill hosted at the Sheraton. Was a small gathering. Twelve, fifteen people. Bill paid a local poet to recite a few poems. Somebody played the piano quietly in the background. Ian was looking the happiest Dale had seen him in a while, except for fleeting moments when his eyes would begin to glance inwards. Loxley walk towards Dale, arms outstretched. Dale fell into them, eyes slowly adjusting themselves to the light. Loxley stroke his face, fingers still warm against Dale's bearded cheeks. Suddenly Dale spring out of his

125

grasp and start off towards the bedroom, both hands clutching his head, his steps unsteady. Loxley follow slowly behind.

'The doctor did say it would happen. Just when him least expected it.' Dale pull on the pair of trousers him did leave next to the dresser last night. 'Just when him think everything all right. Just when him think him getting better. Having the time of his life. Then it would strike. Disabling him even worse than before. Probably putting him into a coma. Probably paralysing him for life. Probably leave him brain dead.'

Dale fish through the dresser for a tee shirt, scattering several on the carpet. Loxley watch silently from the doorway, gown tied securely round his waist, a frown streaking his forehead only partway. His chest didn't rattle as much these days, but purple spots were beginning to fester the lower regions of his back, alongside his arms and neck. They didn't itch or blister or hurt or swell-up, them only cause a slight discolouring to his very pale yellow skin and gave the idea that soon them would cover his entire body. At nights, Dale anoint him with a nasty-smelling potion the doctor prescribe, but just as one spot would disappear, another would show-up elsewhere in much larger proportions. Through the part in the curtain, day was just beginning to streak the sky with assorted shades of red and purple and orange. A dog howled in the distance. Several others follow suit.

'What did the sister say?'

Dale look up, eyes wide, unseeing, as if just noticing Loxley for the first time. Him slip on the tee shirt over his head, arms upwards stretched. 'She think him dead. But him not dead. Him just stiff. That's how him looked the last time at the hospital. But him not dead. Him just look stiff.' Dale pull a shirt from off the wire hanger in the closet, slip it over his shoulders and start to button, fingers fumbling.

'So where is Ian, now?' Loxley walk over to Dale, who was standing by the bed with a pair of shoes hanging over two of his fingers, and start to unbutton Dale's shirt, this time lining up the correct button with the right hole.

Dale drop the shoes on the rug, the socks follow after, noiseless. 'She didn't mention where.' Dale stop. For all of a sudden him couldn't understand . . . Why was Andrea calling? Ian couldn't possibly be at the mother's house again. Dale jerk himself out of Loxley's reach and tuck the shirt hurriedly into the mouth of the trousers.

Ian can't possibly be at the mother's house, again. Not after all that's been happening. Couldn't he just see that him will have to leave her alone for a while? Give her time to heal whatever pain him cause her or she bring on herself. That him can't just bulldoze his way into her life. Obviously she don't want him around. Why bother? Why continue to worry-up himself? Couldn't he learn from the last time, that she'd probably spot him hobbling up to the gate from her window upstairs and dash out the house just in time . . .?

According to Bill, Ian had wanted to tell her about the baptism, to invite her. For several days now, Ian been asking Bill to drop him off at her house. Bill say him wasn't sure. After all he'd been hearing about the woman, him wasn't sure if it was the right thing. But Ian was certain. 'Don't you see Bill, this is exactly what she would've wanted? Me life now turned over for the better. Me soul now given over to Christ. That's what she's always wanted. Now maybe she wouldn't favour Courtney and Andrea so much anymore, now . . .'

Bill agreed then. It was Tuesday. Thursday was the appointed day. Wednesday morning early, must be Ian decide him couldn't wait anymore, him dress himself and quietly creep out the house, the foot of his cane padded wth several pairs of socks which him discard at the side of the house as soon as him was out the gate. It took two hours and three different buses to get to Miss Kaysen's house. By the time Ian arrived in the middle of the afternoon, sweat had washed his brows and him was feeling slightly faint. It was an extremely humid day, no breeze atall was blowing. Garbage pick-up people on strike again, piles of rubbish decorate the roadside, its stench ravage the air. But none of this Ian paid attention to. Him did only have one intention and that was to get to the mother's house. Already in his mouth, rolling back and forth on his tongue, was the entire conversation framed.

First him would knock at the door boldly and Andrea would

run downstairs to let him in. 'Ian!' she would shriek, her eyes cloudy with joy, but him would only wave her oneside with his stick and march right upstairs to his mother's office where she keep the accounts to the eggs and young pullets she sell in tall metallic file cabinets. Him wouldn't pause to run his fingers through the cat's hair as she rub against his calves, or to drink a glass of ice water, or to mop his face, or to smooth out his shirt and tie that had grown dishevelled in the journey, or to tighten his trousers back on to his waist for them'd slide-down to lean on his hips forming a pocket of air on his behind.

Him was on a mission to straighten out things once and for all with his mother. Him would show her the picture of Bill's sister that him have in his wallet. She was a nice-looking light-skinned girl with good hair. Her nose wasn't too broad, it was small and demure and her lips weren't too wide. She didn't have bad skin either, and her teeth were good, not yellow like ripe banana or rotten or missing from the front. His mother would like her rightaway. More so than Courtney's wife, who even though came from a family that owned plenty land, was as black as Ace of Spades.

Then him would let his mother know that as soon as him was back on his two feet, as soon as him was feeling a little strong, which would be in no time atall, as soon as him get back to work (he'd been out now over six months), him would start to make plans for the wedding. Not a grand big thing, him would explain, thin arms outstretched, but a close little gathering with her family, most of whom would be coming from England, a few friends, and of course his own family.

And even before she would be able to digest all of that information, Ian would fumble in his back pockets for the programme, and when his hands come up empty, would search frantically in his side pockets before breathing easy again upon finally retrieving it from his breast pocket. Then him would tell her, slightly breathless, 'Mama, Mama, listen to this. Here,' and him would pick up her round wire-rimmed spectacles from off the desk and hand it to her, 'put on your glasses so you can hear properly.' Then him would swallow, eyes wet with joy, and begin

128

to read aloud from the crisp white piece of paper riddled with folds.

'As God Is My Witness Episcopal Church Wishes To Invite You To Its Baptism Ceremony On Sunday, 25 Of August At Nine O'Clock Sharp. The Following Persons Will Be Cleansed Free Of All Sin And Shame.' Then him would read off all the names and in an even louder voice shout out his. And his mother would be very proud, probably as proud as the time Ian had passed the accounting exam on his first try while Courtney still hadn't passed his the third time, even with all the added tutelage his mother paid for.

So that Wednesday morning, Ian's eyes weren't on the swarm of flies buzzing and having a heyday over the garbage. His nostrils didn't pick up whiffs of funk. Only a rigid determination settle itself on his narrow peanut face, spurring him onwards, back bent slightly forward, storming ahead, feet not as rapid as them clump them way slowly and firm along the boulevard like an old tree.

But when him arrive, the front door was wide open and nobody was home. When him arrive, the transistor radio on top of the old television set was blaring out news of the two gunmen shot and killed by Morant Bay Police, but no one was in earshot. When him arrive and instantly started calling out for Andrea and his mother in his loud hoarse voice, only dull echoes answered. When him arrive and bang on all the doors in the house, knock them open with the foot of his cane and peer in, only the naked room look back at him. Later on that evening, when Miss Dimple and Bill finally found him fast asleep on the bed that used to be his, salty tears dried to his cheeks in flaky streaks, the house was still wide open and empty.

'Dale, why you don't call the mother's house to make sure?' Loxley ask him.

'She doesn't have a phone.'

'Oh.' Loxley sigh and scratch his head.

Sitting on the edge of the bed, Dale start to put on his socks and shoes again. 'Can you drop me up at the public hospital?'

Loxley sit down next to him, sinking the mattress with the

added weight. Him put his hand around Dale's shoulders. 'But you don't know if that's where she call from?' His tone was gentle, patient.

'Listen, you dropping me there or not?' Dale spring around at him, eyes snarling. Him didn't like it when Loxley touch him so intimately. All that was over now.

'Sure.' Loxley leap off the bed and start to put on his clothes. 'It's just funny that she would call. I mean that Ian would call her first. I mean that she would be the first to know if Ian dead or not.' Loxley sigh out loud. 'Maybe we should call Ian's apartment first, just to check, then the hospital.'

Dale didn't stop him. It was getting more and more complicated. Why was Andrea calling? She wasn't even at the party. It was Dale and Ian who shared a taxi back from the hotel. And then Dale did ask the driver to please not drive off until the light went on in Ian's bedroom. Then Dale came home. Unless of course, Ian went back out. Two o'clock this morning, him call a cab and drive over to the mother's house. Probably because it was his birthday, his twenty-fourth birthday.

'Well, nobody's at Ian's house.' Loxley walk back into the room and handed Dale a cup of mint tea. Dale was still sitting at the edge of the bed, both hands holding up his head. Him tell Loxley thanks and rest the mug on the floor by his shoes. 'The receptionist's going to check and call me back.'

Dale nod and get up off the bed. Head towards the door.

'Where you going?'

'To make a call.'

'Now? Who you calling?'

Dale pause, take a deep breath. 'I going to call Nevin.'

'Nevin?'

'Yes.' Dale's voice was low, restrained. 'I going to call Nevin.'

'What Nevin have to do with any of this? I thought you say him wasn't at the party. That him and Ian not really friends anymore. What happens if the receptionist call back?'

Dale didn't answer. Him feel his temper mounting. If Loxley open his mouth one more time, him was just going to cancel the plans to get a three-bedroom apartment together. Or leave. Do something. Him can't stand this blasted jealousy business anymore. Loxley should stop it. They weren't lovers anymore. Things had changed.

Dale dial the number that was so familiar to him. Him thought about Nevin's eyes in the dream, red with anger, charging towards him. Dale shudder. Him wanted to tell Nevin about the dream, to tell him about Ian, to ask him to help take care of everything, for him was so good that way. Would know the correct things to say that would calm Dale, that would smooth-out the situation, that would give Dale added strength to go on. Dale could imagine Nevin tossed crossway the bed, sheets every which way, a slice of white peeping from his eyes where the lids don't fold over completely, the centipede by his mouth raising with each intake of breath.

Then the phone would ring and him would utter out some nonsense or other, part of a dream. The phone would ring again. And this time him would curse out loud and reach over to the side of the bed to pick it from the cradle but his heavy arms would knock over a glass of water, the alarm clock, his pipe, and him would curse again just before him mumble hello into the phone. The phone rang seven, eight, nine times. And when the voice finally crackle into the receiver, it wasn't Nevin's tone him hear, but a much deeper bass tempo. Dale hang up sudden, tears bubbling beneath the surface of his eyes.

Then the phone rang again, chiming loud into the stillness of the morning, and it was the receptionist calling to say there was no sign of an Ian Kaysen anywhere atall in the hospital. Loxley put down the receiver silently. It was three-thirty.

'Well, come, let us go over to the mother's house.' Loxley grab the sweater hanging from the hook on the door.

'No.' Dale sat down back on the couch, hands folded crossway hugging his chest, his shoulders. For all of a sudden, Miss Kaysen's pig eyes gleaming with hate jumped before him, and him just couldn't bear the thought of going back to her house, to watch her sparkling white teeth spew bile, to inhale the stench of hate exuding from her house frock.

'Look, I want to help you out, for you nervous, it's a stressful time. But you not giving me the chance.' Loxley's voice sounded tired.

'I don't need your help.'

'What!'

'I don't need your help.' Dale's eyes were flashing, the crab trembling slightly. Him wonder whose voice that was now, the person who replace him or . . .

'Here, take the car.' Loxley fling down the car key on the couch towards Dale. 'Maybe it's not such a good idea to live together after all.' And him march back into the bedroom and slam the door loud behind him.

During the long drive to Miss Kaysen's house, Dale didn't want to think. Him know it was the stroke, it had to be the stroke again. The doctor say it would come. No doubt the mother said something to upset Ian and it brought on the stroke. But that didn't mean it was the end. That him was dead. The clock on the dashboard glowed four thirty. Dale wonder if him should stop and call Nevin again. These days at least once a day the urge to hear Nevin's deep baritone would often overcome him. Usually after Nevin left notes for him at the post office, which Dale would always pick up, but never read, but not always. Sometimes the urge comes on its own accord. And Dale would have to get up and get dressed and leave the house. Walk for a long time, head bowed, kicking pebbles, crying desperately. Disappointed at the shape of his life. He'd left the church completely now. At first him would miss one or two Sundays in a row, then one morning, him just decided never to go back.

During the mornings before work, him volunteer at a Youth centre not far from Loxley's apartment. There for several hours, him teach small boys and girls to play cricket and swim. On weekends, when Loxley wasn't working, Dale would prepare picnic baskets and the two would go off on day trips, sometimes mountain climbing, other times fishing or scuba diving. During those times Dale would feel a twinge of deep affection, something similar to what him would feel for Nevin. But quickly him would squelch it, reminding himself that this sibling-like relationship was easier. It would last longer. Wouldn't hurt as much. Sometimes Dale spent time with Loxley's friends, other times him would go

132

and visit his Aunt Daisy. Religiously now, every fortnight him travel the long five-hour bus ride back to country where him clear away the weeds that grow around his mother's tomb in the Parish cemetery.

Although Dale couldn't bring himself to start smoking, him did buy a large hardcover book on pipes, which him keep on the centre table in the living room and browse through now and again. Dale start to drink whiskey sours though, and would often order them at the bar, nursing the glass the way Nevin would. Sometimes Dale would glimpse Nevin at the bar and the knot (generally at ease in his belly) would suddenly fly up to his chest and stay there until Dale have to get up and leave, eyes wet. Nevin still wear the cast. Going six months now. Dale did hear that there was an accident the same night Nevin drop off the fat white parcel. Drunk driving. Car spin off the road and turn over. Dale hear too that Rose got married to the Rastaman, Barry, and had moved out. Was now expecting.

As the car ease silently down the empty road, Dale could hear the wet morning call of baby swallows flying across the sky. Now and again, him spot a Robin Red Breast, a wren. Thin yellow streaks of sunshine were just beginning to glisten over tree tops and there was a purity in the air, the tender sky. Grass and flowers glisten with the sheen of early morning dew. It wasn't altogether light when Dale pull up the car at the gate, but him could make out the gleaming steel of the silver padlock and the shape of Andrea's long white nightie bobbing timidly about her legs as she pace back and forth. It was still cool, and the brilliant face of the moon was just starting to fade, to make room for the yellow sun.

'Oh, Dale.'

Her voice was hoarse and him wrap his heavy arms around her thin and trembling shoulders, his chin nestled in the deep grooves of her collar.

'It's OK, Andrea. It's OK.' Him try to pacify her with the deep reassuring bass of his voice, his right hand making circular motions around her frail back. 'You send for the doctor, already?'

'Oh, Dale.'

And Dale took that as yes, and pull her even closer against his

133

massive chest, as she shower down more warm tears into the wide neck of his sweater.

'Andrea, all we can do is pray. The doctors try them best. Did everything they could. But this thing, this disease,' him hated to call it that, 'is out of our hands all together. Out of our hands. Out of our hands.' Him repeat the phrase over and over, liking more and more the silk tones of his own deep voice in the stillness of the morning air, and its effect on Andrea, whose trembling was starting to ease, whose tears were starting to subside. Slowly him loosen his grip on her shoulders, and brush away strands of straightened hair that had fallen across her peanut-shaped face, hiding wet eyes.

'What time Ian came over?' A white furry cat circled its tail around the two pairs of feet, rubbed its head gently against Dale's ankle. Dale eased away the cat gently with the sharp tips of his shoes.

'Bout three.' She was whispering as if afraid others might be listening. 'Him was knocking on the door because him never have any keys. Oh God, Dale. Him dead. I know him dead.'

'Shhh. Shhh.' Dale put his forefinger on her lip. Tears were beginning to fall again. 'It's all right. Him did look dead when I saw him at the hospital too, but that don't mean anything. Doctors know what to do.'

'But Dale, she push him.'

'What you mean push him?' His eyes widen. 'Who, you mother?'

And the weeping start up afresh and the tears tumbled from her eyes.

'You mother push him, Andrea?' But only tears answered.

'Andrea, you mother push him? Andrea?' His voice was gaining in momentum and the fear that did grip his shoulders earlier on, started to inflict pain again.

'Andrea, listen to me. Andrea?' His voice was rasp against the bitter chill of the morning.

'I heard the knocking first. And so I push up the window to find out who it was. It was him. And I told him to hold on, mind him wake up Mama, I coming down.' She pause to blow her nose inside her dress. 'Same time Mama got up and ask me who I talking to. I tell her Ian. She didn't know who Ian was, Dale.'

Andrea pause again, searching inwards for strength to continue on with her story.

Dale didn't know what to say. Him could feel his own strength slipping away gradually. His fingers slacken from around Andrea's thin coffee-coloured neck. Him feel his stomach tremble from fatigue and lack of food. Him feel his knees weaken, badly wanting to buckle inside his trousers.

' "Ian, who?" she ask me.

' "Mama, Ian. Our Ian."

'And she didn't remember, Dale. She ask me if it was Ian Fenns. The man who come to do work on the house now and again. And why him was downstairs pounding like that. This hour of the morning. And I say no, it's your son, Ian. And all this time, Ian was still downstairs pounding on the door, knocking on the windows, calling out Mama. And she look at me, Dale. Look at me and tell me she didn't have a son named Ian. And why the hell I was playing the fool with her at this hour of the morning. And then she went back into her room and bolt the door behind her. And of course Ian was still downstairs pounding on the door, calling out Mama. So I run down and open the door and Ian was crying, saying it was his birthday, and Mama didn't even send him a card. And him had a whole plastic bag full of letters in his hands. And him was going up towards Mama's room, and I tell him not to wake her now, to come upstairs with me and wait till morning. But him wouldn't listen, and was still crying, saying how it was his birthday and scattering all the envelopes with her handwriting over the floor.

'And him start to bang on her door, Dale, asking where was the card. And I try to pull him away from the door, but him only push me oneside. And then Mama start to unfasten the bolt on her door, and I scream at him to move, Dale, to move from the door, but him wouldn't listen . . .'

And at that point, Dale couldn't listen anymore. For him could just see Ian, standing uncertain by her door, rank with the smell of smoke and sweat from the party, the padded shoulders of his black silk suit concealing the frail thinness of his limbs, hooded eyes brilliant with pain.

Then Miss Kaysen would swing the door to her room wide open

135

and the bright light would blind him for a few minutes, then his eyes would adjust. And him would step back a little, for her tallness would've caught him off balance, or maybe the ferocious wind of her breath. Then the two, of similar length and breadth, would meet eye to eye, shoulder to shoulder. And Ian would see the fiery charcoal of his eyes reflected in hers. And him would see his own hollow cheeks, and triangular chin, and pointed ears, and tender lips and tendrils of laugh lines spreading by the mouth corners, imprinted on her spindly face, hardened by rough life.

'Mama.' And maybe him would start to cry, silent, salty tears of relief and love that temporarily blur his vision and fill his heart.

'Get out.' And the hardness of her voice would stop him dead in his tracks, and his outstretched arms ready to pull her to his chest, would waver uncertainly around him. And the tears bubbled up on the surface of his eyes, would remain locked in place, refusing to bubble over and spill.

'Get out.' And maybe she took one step forward, the red house-coat girthed tight around her waist billowing around her spindly little legs, and maybe Ian, surprised, took one step backward, his heels, forgetting altogether that they'd reached the tip of the step, tilted backwards, off balance, for it'd been so long since he'd set foot in that house.

'Get out.' And maybe she took one step forward, the red house-coat girthed tight around her waist billowing around her spindly little legs, and chucked him in the chest with both of her hands clamp shut into fists, and maybe the wind flew out of Ian's chest, and his heels forgetting altogether that they'd reached the tip of the step, tilted backwards, off balance, for it'd been so long since he'd set foot in that house.

'Get out.' And maybe she took one step forward, the red house-coat girthed tight around her waist billowing around her spindly little legs, raise up her hands to chuck, but Ian catch them and clasp them together just in time, and maybe she pushed against him to set her free, the firewood smoke of her breath, breathing hard in his ears, and maybe him push back against her for it'd been so long since him feel her thin tender arms holding him so close, and maybe in that short quick moment him inhale the scent of stale milk from her tender little breasts and the scent of sweat

136

from underneath her arms and behind her ears, and the scent of coconut oil in her hair, and olive oil on her skin, and maybe him could hear the soft cooing of her voice, as she whisper some song or other under her breath, strong with the scent of parched coffee beans or roasted almond nuts or pounded black pepper from seasoned meat.

And maybe she too would remember the pretty little boy, lying quiet in her arms, sucking tenderly on her breasts, making gurgling sounds, head full of curly jet black hair, cheeks chiselled just like his grandfather's but soft like velvet and warm like the sea. And the brilliant starlets of his eyes staring rigidly at her breasts would bring to mind the sightless eyes of her own mother. And maybe she would push back against Ian, for the memory was too tremendous, and his heels forgetting altogether that they'd reached the tip of the step, tilted backwards, off balance, for it'd been so long since he'd set foot in that house.

But Andrea was starting to weep again, her fingers clawing at his chest even harder, and Ian was inside stretch-out dead, his face still, a tiny gash on his forehead where it hit the concrete at the foot of the stairs, and Miss Kaysen was walking toward them, swaying smoothly in a blood red house-coat with fur on the arms where it circle her wrists, and fur on the bottom where it swill around her ankles and fur on the collar where it envelop her slender stately neck. And that was where Dale's eyes stayed, on the fur on the collar where it envelop her slender stately neck, unable to bring them to meet her face, as Andrea slipped slowly from his hands and crumple into a neat little pile by his feet, and Miss Kaysen walked slowly towards him.